HOWDY!

Welcome to the Circle C. My name is Andi Carter. If you are a new reader, here's a quick roundup of my family, friends, and adventures:

I'm a tomboy who lives on a huge cattle ranch near Fresno, California, in the exciting 1880s. I would rather ride my palomino mare, Taffy, than do anything else. I mean well, but trouble just seems to follow me around.

Our family includes my mother Elizabeth, my ladylike older sister Melinda, and my three older brothers: Justin (a lawyer), Chad, and Mitch. I love them, but sometimes they treat me like a pest. My father was killed in a ranch accident a few years ago.

In **Long Ride Home**, Taffy is stolen and it's my fault. I set out to find my horse and end up far from home and in a heap of trouble.

In **Dangerous Decision**, I nearly trample my new teacher in a horse race with my friend Cory. Later, I have to make a life-or-death choice.

Next, I discover I'm the only one who doesn't know the Carter **Family Secret**, and it turns my world upside down.

In **San Francisco Smugglers**, a flood sends me to school in the city for two months. My new roommate, Jenny, and I discover that the little Chinese servant-girl in our school is really a slave.

Trouble with Treasure is what Jenny, Cory, and I find when we head into the mountains with Mitch to pan for gold.

Later, I may lose my beloved horse, Taffy, if I tell what I saw in **Price of Truth**.

So now, saddle up and ride into my latest adventure!

Andi

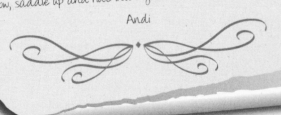

ANDREA CARTER AND THE

Trouble with Treasure

To:
Mrs.
McHattie

Adventure
Awaits!

Susan Marlow

The Circle C Adventures Series

ANDREA CARTER AND THE

Trouble with Treasure

Susan K. Marlow

Kregel
Publications

Andrea Carter and the Trouble with Treasure

© 2010 by Susan K. Marlow

Published by Kregel Publications, a division of Kregel, Inc., P.O. Box 2607, Grand Rapids, MI 49501.

ISBN 978-0-8254-3352-8

Printed in the United States of America

10 11 12 13 14 / 5 4 3 2 1

Chapter One

THE MAP

San Joaquin Valley, California, Early Summer 1881

A blast of hot summer air struck thirteen-year-old Andi Carter as she led her palomino mare, Taffy, from the barn. She'd been looking forward to the ride into Fresno this afternoon, but now the thought of climbing on a horse and galloping around in this heat made her reconsider. Already she felt rivulets of sweat trickling down the back of her neck.

"Is it always this hot around here?" Jenny Grant's voice sounded pained.

Andi stopped in her tracks and turned to face her friend, who was leading a pinto pony a few steps behind Taffy. The girl's face was nearly as red as her fiery hair, which was pulled back into a long, tight braid. In the two weeks since Jenny came to the Circle C, dozens of new freckles had popped out and covered not only her nose and cheeks, but also her forehead and chin. The California sun did not suit Jenny at all.

Andi grinned at her friend's flushed appearance. "It's barely June. You should be here for August. Then you'd know what hot *really* feels like." She pulled her wide-brimmed hat forward to shade her eyes. It offered some protection from the glaring sun but none from the heat. "Don't you have summer where you're from?"

Jenny squinted up at the sun. "Not like this. During those rare days when the sun does start blistering me, I run down to the dock and jump in the bay. There's nothing like a ducking to cool a body off good and proper. And we have trees so tall and cool just a stone's throw away." She gave Andi a weak smile. "Not many places to cool off around here, are there?"

"Nope," Andi confessed, "I'm afraid not." She looked around the yard and tried to imagine the tall fir trees of Washington Territory standing in place of the scattered valley oaks around her ranch house and outbuildings. "You get used to it, I reckon." In spite of the heat, she shivered at the thought of cooling off in any body of water larger than a creek.

Jenny raked a sleeve across her forehead, jammed the black felt hat Andi had lent her onto her head, and sighed. "Well, I don't want to stand around jawing all day. Let's go."

"It's a long, hot ride to town," Andi said. "Are you sure you want to go? Maybe we should stick close to the ranch and wait for Mitch to take us up in the hills. It'll be cooler there, and you'll feel at home. Lots of mountains and pine trees up at that logging camp."

Jenny wrinkled her forehead. "I've seen my share of logging camps." She clambered into the saddle on Patches' back and secured the reins. "If I don't see the town this week, then I'll miss it completely. Soon as we get back from our trek into the hills, it'll be time for me to pack up and head home." She took a deep breath and set her jaw. "If this heat ain't gonna bother you, then it ain't gonna bother me, neither."

Jenny lapsed into speech Andi recognized as her friend's I'm-getting-impatient talk. No matter how hard Jenny Grant tried to walk and talk like a lady, she couldn't seem to shake her thirteen years of living in the company of loggers in the middle of nowhere. Not even a year at a fancy San Francisco girls' school had done much to curb Jenny's wild ways.

Andi was glad it hadn't. She liked Jenny's carefree and sometimes reckless view of life. Why, next to Jenny Grant, Andi appeared almost a lady! She muffled a giggle and mounted Taffy. "All right, let's go see the town."

The two horses were in no mood to hurry in the heat, so Andi let Taffy have her head, and Jenny followed suit. The ride to town—normally an hour's trip—took longer than Andi liked. By the time they plodded down the dusty street and dismounted in front of Goodwin's Mercantile, Andi and Jenny were drenched in sweat and their canteens were empty. Andi knew the horses must be thirsty too.

They had no sooner led Taffy and Patches to the watering trough when Andi heard a familiar shout.

"Andi!" Cory Blake skidded to a stop beside the girls. He was waving a yellowed piece of paper in his hand. "You won't believe what Ollie traded me. Look here. It's a . . ." He paused at the look on Andi's face and frowned. "What's wrong?"

Andi let Taffy finish her drink, then wrapped her mare's reins around the hitching rail a few yards away. She hadn't seen Cory since last February, when the town had been overrun by three flooding creeks. Instead of a holiday, Andi had been shipped off to school in San Francisco to finish out the winter term. She'd also decided to stay for the spring term. She was home at last, and here Cory was, waving a dirty old paper in her face and acting like he'd seen her only yesterday.

"No 'Howdy-Andi-glad-you're-back-how-was-the-city'?" she said when she returned to the trough.

Cory pulled off his hat and gave her a cocky smile. "Howdy, Andi. Glad you're back. How was the city? Hope you didn't pick up any snooty ways at that fancy school you went to." He shoved his hat back on his blond head and turned his attention to the paper clutched in his hand. "Now take a look at—"

"You must be Cory." Jenny grasped Cory's hand and pumped it. Her words tumbled out. "I'm Jenny. Jenny Grant. I'm staying with Andi for a few weeks. We were roommates at school. I heard lots about you. Sounds like you have fine times around these parts—fishing and racing your horses and playing ball. Nice to meet you."

Cory threw Andi a helpless look.

"That's what happens when you're in such an all-fired hurry to blab about your latest scheme instead of showing my guest some manners," Andi said with a smirk.

Cory slid his hand free from Jenny's sweaty grasp and wiped it on his britches. "Pleased t' meet you, Jenny," he said with a red face. Some of his enthusiasm had drained away.

Andi dipped her hand in the horse trough and swirled the tepid water around. "So, what did Ollie trade you?"

Cory's face broke into a wide smile, and he settled himself on the edge of the trough. "Well, Ollie's pa works at the land office, you know. They got some new survey maps in to replace the old, outdated ones, and"—he smoothed the paper across his knees—"I traded Ollie five aggie marbles, the largest toad in Fresno County, and two genuine arrowheads for this old map." He held it out for Andi to see.

Jenny peered over Andi's shoulder. "What do you want with an outdated map? Looks to me like the waste of a good toad."

"My thoughts exactly," Andi said with a giggle.

"Look here," Cory persisted. "It's an old survey map of the area up around Fresno Flats. See all these symbols? They show gold diggings and claims that folks don't bother about any longer. I suppose there's a working mine or two up on Potter's Ridge, but most folks around those parts are ranching or logging now. The little diggings are likely all played out and no good to anybody." He craned his head to catch the sudden interest in Andi's blue eyes.

"You thinking of prospecting for gold?" she asked.

"Maybe." Cory tapped the map with his finger. "This shows places along creeks where gold was found years and years ago. Seems to me a fella could nose around, dig a shovel into the creek bed, slosh it around a bit, and see what he could find." He gave Andi a sly grin. "Remember that fella who found the forty-ounce gold nugget in Coarse Gold Gulch? He was purely lucky, that's all. Why not take a couple of weeks and see what kind of treasure *I* can find?"

Andi snatched the map from Cory's hand and peered at it. It was faded and partially smeared, but words like "Willow Creek," "Grub Gulch," "Potter Ridge Mine," and "McFarland's Ranch" filled the spaces, along with tiny drawings of pickaxes scattered here and there along the curved and twisted contour lines. A dotted line with the word "flume" snaked its way across the page.

Jenny traced the flume symbol with her finger. "I know what *this* is. Loggers send timber down from the mountains in a flume. Saves a heap of time, instead of using horses and wagons." She squinted at the tiny print. "Looks like this one goes clear up to the . . . the Sugar Pine logging camp." She looked at Andi. "Say, isn't that the name of the camp your brother's taking us up to see?"

Andi nodded and handed the map back to Cory. "Tell you what, Cory. Mitch is heading up to that very logging camp next week, and he's taking Jenny and me along. I had to do some mighty fine sweet-talking, but he agreed that Jenny should see all of California that she can before she goes home. If we happen to stumble across any gold on the way, I'll tell you about it." She grinned at the look on her friend's face. "What's the matter?"

"You're going *here*?" He thumped the paper. "Right past all those swell gold diggings? You taking the stage or packing in on horses?"

"Packing in, of course. It's going to be fun. Just Mitch, Jenny, and me for two whole weeks on the trail. I can't wait."

Cory wagged his head. He carefully folded the map, secured it in his trouser pocket, and said, "Do you suppose Mitch would like another fella along on that trip to keep him company?"

Andi considered. She looked from Jenny to Cory and then at the sliver of paper peeking out from Cory's pocket. "I'll ask Mitch," she finally said, "and you ask your folks. But"—she pointed at Cory's pocket—"any gold you find with that map we split three ways: you, me, and Jenny. Deal?" She reached out her hand.

Cory's eyes gleamed as he took her hand. "It's a deal," he said in a low voice, "but we've got to keep this to ourselves. No telling what would happen if word leaked out about our treasure hunt."

"Why are you whispering?" Andi asked. "There's nobody around but us and the horses."

"You can't be too careful," he replied with a shrug.

"You can't be too careful about what?" a new voice echoed from the mercantile doorway. Jack Goodwin strolled out from his father's store, sucking on an ice chip. The screen door slammed shut behind him as he joined Andi and her friends around the watering trough. Smacking his lips, he sat next to Cory, brushed his unruly dark hair from his eyes, and repeated, "You can't be too careful about what?"

"Treasure," Andi said, swallowing hard. That ice chip sure looked good! "Cory thinks he's found another get-rich-quick scheme. Want to hear about it?"

She knew what Jack's answer would be. A few years ago, Cory had talked Jack into helping him with an idea to swipe ice from the Goodwin's ice house and sell it door to door. Trouble was, by the time they reached the fourth house, the ice had melted into a puddle in the bucket. When Mr. Goodwin found out, both boys got their backsides warmed. More than likely, Jack wouldn't want to join Cory in another fool notion to get rich.

She was right.

Jack snorted. "A treasure hunt? Not me, Cory. I'm not fool enough to follow a phony map some shyster sold you." He finished his ice chip and ran the back of his hand across his wet lips.

"Get us some ice, Jack," Andi pleaded. If she didn't get something cool inside pretty quick, she was going to melt. "My guest isn't used to this kind of heat."

For the first time, Jack looked at Jenny. Andi made a quick introduction and repeated her request. "Your pa won't mind. I'm sure he won't."

"I've got a better way to cool off," Jack said. He shot a glance at Jenny, who looked like she was sweltering. Then he twisted around, leaned over the horse trough, and plunged his head in.

Andi gasped. "Jack!"

"He's plumb crazy," Jenny said, laughing.

Jack pulled his head from the trough. Dark hair plastered his forehead and over his ears. Water streamed down his face. "That's what I call cooling off."

Andi wasn't convinced. "That's disgusting—that dirty old horse water. Taffy used it ten minutes ago."

Jack wiped his face and laughed. "Well, I'm not *drinking* it, Andi. Besides, I watched them fill it not more than an hour ago. Your horses were the first ones to drink from it. It's as clean as the water from our kitchen pump." He reached into the trough and tossed a handful of water in Andi's face.

Andi sputtered and leaped up. "That's not funny, Jack!"

"But you gotta admit it felt good—near as good as an ol' ice chip, I bet."

Andi bit back the rest of her reply. Yes, it *had* felt good. She looked at Jenny. Her friend was gazing longingly at the cool water. Andi turned back to Jack. "You sure it's clean?"

At Jack's nod, Andi leaned over and splashed the cool water against her face. Jenny joined her and let out a sigh as the water dribbled down her cheeks. "This is pure heaven." Then she leaned close to Andi and whispered, "I'm hot enough to pull that trick your friend did. My head's burning up."

Jack whooped. "I heard that, Jenny, and I got an idea. How 'bout a head-ducking contest? See who can keep his head under the longest." He didn't wait for Jenny's answer, but turned to Cory. "You game?"

Cory's blue-gray eyes glinted in fun. "I'm game. How 'bout you, Andi?"

Andi bit her lip in indecision. Last summer she would have joined in without hesitation. But she was thirteen years old now—too old to be playing foolish games with the town boys, even if they were good friends she'd known for years. Wading in the creek, yes. Splashing in the town's fountain, maybe. But ducking her head in a horse trough in the middle of the street? For once, she decided to think before she acted. She shook her head. "No, I'd better not."

"Well," Jenny said, "I'm game." She tossed her hat aside.

"You don't have to live here," Andi said. "Nobody knows you. But me? Everybody around these parts knows my family. I don't want to give the town gossips an excuse to wag their tongues." She sighed. "I reckon I'll sit this one out."

Cory shrugged. "Suit yourself. I guess you can judge who wins."

"I can do that. Then Jenny and I will be on our way. I'm showing her the town." She stared at the still water and said, "You ready?"

Jenny, Cory, and Jack leaned over the horse trough as one. "We're ready," Jenny said.

At Andi's shout of "Go!" the three contestants plunged their heads deep into the water. She counted slowly and waited for the first head to pop up. "Thirty, thirty-one . . ." she continued counting. Would they never come up for air? Andi was suddenly glad she'd refused to participate. She liked to win, but she'd have had no chance in this contest. She couldn't hold her breath so long.

With a gasp, Cory's blond head flew from the trough. His heaving chest and soaking wet shirt threw water droplets everywhere. He coughed and sputtered. A second later, Jack was coughing and sucking in air. Then Jenny emerged, tossing her long braid—wet from its dunking—back and forth. She straightened up, gulping air.

"That was mighty fine!" she said when she caught her breath.

"You won," Andi said, "but not by much. You three cooler now?" She settled herself on the edge of the trough and gazed at the cool water. She splashed a handful on her face. It helped a little, but she wished . . .

"You look mighty hot, Andi."

She turned in time to hear Cory shout, "No, Jack!" Then she felt a push and tumbled backwards into the trough.

The shock of the cool water didn't douse Andi's fury. She sat up, sputtering her anger and dismay. She was soaked now—from head to toe. Sitting in the watering trough, she would soon become the laughing stock of the town. It was time to mount Taffy and head for home before any of the town biddies saw her. Jenny would have to set aside her sightseeing of Fresno.

She gripped the edges of the trough and struggled to stand up. Cory reached out a helping hand, but Andi slapped it aside. "Some friend *you* are. Why didn't you keep Jack from dunking me?"

Jenny rushed to Cory's defense. "It happened too fast." She glared at Jack. "You remind me of my brother Eli—playing no-good jokes on folks."

Jack didn't flinch at Jenny's rebuke. "Sorry, Andi. I didn't mean no harm. You got wet. So what? Climb out, and I'll ask Pa for some licorice."

Andi ignored Jack's half-baked apology and clambered over the side of the trough. She didn't want any licorice. Getting out of town unseen was the only thing on her mind right now. "Come on, Jenny."

Too late. A man's voice stopped her cold.

"What in blazes is going on here?"

Chapter Two

UNDER ARREST

A ndi turned and came face to face with Fresno's new young deputy, Hugh Baker. Her heart skipped a beat.

"I asked you a question," Hugh snapped. "What's going on?" He bored into her with a dark, impatient glare. His deputy's badge flashed in the sunlight.

Instead of answering, Andi looked at her friends. They stood stock-still on the other side of the horse trough, looking every bit as frightened as Andi felt. It was no secret that Deputy Baker stalked the streets, looking for an excuse to round up would-be troublemakers. She had listened to more than one conversation around the supper table lately about the cocky new deputy. Her brothers didn't like him at all. And no wonder. New to his job and trying to impress his boss, he'd arrested more folks in the six weeks he'd been deputy than Sheriff Tate arrested in six months.

Andi didn't want to be next.

A sudden grip on her arm wrenched Andi from her thoughts. "You deaf, girl? Answer me."

"I-I fell in. That's all."

Hugh snorted his disbelief and flicked his gaze to the others. "You three, get over here."

Jenny, Cory, and Jack hurried into the street and stood next to Andi.

"You know good and well the ordinance against messin' with the livestock troughs, especially during the hot months. The sheriff's office got a number of complaints about this very thing. It ain't fittin' to use the troughs for bathing pools or any other shenanigans, you hear?"

Four heads bobbed up and down.

"This trough is on its last leg, and now it's leakin' all over the place."

Andi glanced behind her shoulder. Although she couldn't imagine how it might have happened, a number of small cracks were oozing water. It wouldn't be long before the trough was completely empty.

"It won't happen again," Cory said. "We'll fix it right away. I'll run get the tools."

Hugh shook his head. "I'm taking you four in. You'll sit in the sheriff's office while I round up your folks."

"You mean you're *arresting* us?" Jenny squeaked.

The deputy smirked. "Yep. The town's getting a new water trough from the fines your folks will be paying."

Andi didn't care about the fines. She didn't care about the small crowd of curious bystanders that had gathered on the boardwalk. She only cared about being arrested and sitting in the sheriff's office.

With a sinking heart, she remembered her brother Chad's story of how the deputy had arrested Tom Stringer and Zeke Hollister for painting the drayman's gray horse a bright red in the middle of the night. It wasn't like it hadn't happened before. The drayman usually complained, the artists paid the five-dollar fine, and the *Fresno Expositor* had news for an otherwise dull edition of the paper. But this time Deputy Baker had locked the rowdies up, hoping Mr. Anderson would press serious charges. Andi had laughed, but Chad hadn't intended the story to be funny. Now she understood. The horse-painting incident suddenly didn't sound funny to her, either. Seeing Hugh Baker up close, Andi felt sorry for Tom and Zeke.

She felt sorry for herself.

Andi and her friends shuffled along behind Deputy Baker, heads down. The crowd had grown to at least a dozen townsfolk. Most shook their heads and murmured assurances.

"Russ will set things right, so don't you kids worry none," someone shouted.

Andi sure *hoped* Sheriff Tate would step in and rescue them. It wasn't like they'd broken any *real* law . . . or had they?

"Hugh, ain't you got nothing better to do than arrest decent folks' kids?" another man complained.

A few folks, on the other hand, applauded the deputy's decision. "It's about time somebody tries to corral the town's troublemakers."

Hugh's supporters were Mr. Evans, the undertaker, and his gossipy wife. The old couple never had a good word to say about the youth of Fresno. Andi tried to put as much distance between herself and the undertaker's family as she would an ornery rattlesnake. One never knew when Mr. or Mrs. Evans would strike. *No doubt Mrs. Evans will tattle to Mother,* Andi thought with a sigh.

Mr. Evans stood along the street, giving hearty approval to Hugh's recent arrest. In his "proper" black suit and top hat, he looked ridiculously out of place in the heat. He crossed his arms over his chest and nodded while the kids trooped past.

By the time Hugh herded them into the sheriff's office, Andi's heart was racing. In spite of the sweat trickling down the back of her neck, a cold, hard lump had settled in her stomach.

Hugh shut the door. "Here we are. Make yourselves at home while I fill out the paperwork." He strolled across the tiny office and plunked down in the chair behind the sheriff's desk. He pulled open a drawer, pawed through it, then slammed it shut. "There's got to be a pencil around here somewhere," he muttered.

Andi glanced at her friends. They hadn't moved since entering the office. No one had said a word. Andi gathered up her courage and asked, "When can we see the sheriff?"

Andi liked Sheriff Tate. His honesty and his easy-going manner made him a favorite with the citizens of Fresno—young and old alike. Only real law-breakers feared him. Andi knew she and her friends would get a fair shake from the sheriff. He'd give them a piece of his mind and send them on their way with the promise that their folks would soon hear what had happened. That would be the end of it . . . at least until Andi got home.

Her heart slowed down. The icy lump in her stomach began to melt. Yes, Sheriff Tate would fix things up fine.

Hugh found a pencil stub and began scribbling on a piece of paper. "Huh? What did you say?"

"I want to know when we can talk to Sheriff Tate," Andi said. *You're just the deputy and haven't got much say,* she added silently. She didn't dare say it aloud.

"Sheriff ain't here," Hugh answered without looking up. "Gone to Merced for a couple o' days. Left me in charge." His voice held a hint of gloating as he continued to scribble.

Andi exchanged a worried glance with Cory. *Now what?*

Hugh looked up. He pointed the stubby pencil at Andi and said, "If you kids think you're going to bleat to Sheriff Tate about this, you got another think coming. It's my duty to arrest folks who disturb the peace, start fights, shoot each other, rob banks, spit on the boardwalk, and engage in disorderly contact. I'm charging you four with just that—disorderly conduct and destroying public property. I'm writing up the official charges, and the judge will be seeing you sometime next week about the fines. This time there ain't no sheriff around to overrule me."

Andi felt sick. Cory and Jack groaned. Jenny squeezed Andi's hand and whispered, "Can he do that? I thought we were going up in the hills with Mitch next week."

"He can do it," Jack said sourly. "He's mean enough to do it, too."

"You got something to say, boy?" Hugh snapped.

"No, sir," Jack said.

Andi saw he was shaking with the injustice of it all. She was shaking too. This spiteful, meaner-than-a-cornered rattlesnake of a deputy was fixing to ruin all of Andi and Jenny's plans, and there wasn't a thing she could do about it. It was such a stupid charge.

"I thought you were going to find our folks," Cory said. "I'd just as soon get this over with quick. I'm tired of waiting." To prove his point, he put his hands in his pockets and leaned against the door. "I got things to do."

That was a brave thing to say, Andi thought.

The deputy shoved the chair back and rose to his full height. He wasn't much taller than Cory, but he seemed a lot bigger with the holster around his middle and his deputy's badge glimmering. "Oh, you do, do you?" With a great show of bluster, he stomped across the office and yanked a large ring of keys from a hook. "You four come with me."

Andi looked at the metal ring. She knew what the keys were for—the jail cells. She gasped and burst out, "You can't lock us in a cell. It's . . . it's . . ." She faltered. She wasn't sure why he couldn't do it. She only knew it wasn't right.

"It's unconstitutional," Jack finished.

Everybody stared at Jack. Andi was surprised he knew the word. Jack wasn't the best scholar in the Fresno grammar school.

The deputy gave the kids an amused grin. He motioned them to follow him. "Fine. You show me in the Constitution where it says I can't lock you up, and I'll be happy to abide by it." He marched them down a dim hallway and unlocked a large cell. "Until then . . . in you go."

The cell door slammed shut. The key rattled in the lock. Hugh's grin turned into a chuckle. "That should bring you kids down a peg or two." He twirled the ring of keys. "Don't go away now. I'll be right back. Soon as I get my paper and pencil I'll take your names. Then you can cool your heels in here while I track down your folks."

Andi slumped onto one of the cots in the otherwise bare cell. "You didn't have to lock us up, Deputy. We would've stayed put until you brought our folks."

"So *you* say," Hugh replied. "This way I ain't taking any chances."

The deputy sauntered down the hall and into the office. The door clicked shut behind him.

As soon as Deputy Baker disappeared, Jack gripped the bars of the cell and pushed his face up against them. "I think we're in trouble." He rattled the door and stepped back. "Yep. A *heap* of trouble."

"At least it's nice and cool in here," Jenny said. She sat down next to Andi and leaned back against the cold brick wall.

Andi shivered. To her it was a mite *too* cold. Her wet riding skirt clung to her legs. Her feet sloshed around in her boots. She removed one boot and turned it upside down. Water drizzled onto the floor in a puddle. She glared at Jack. "This is your fault, you know." She took off her other boot and dumped the water out. Then she replaced her boots, stood up, and stamped her feet into place. It didn't help much.

Jack turned from the bars and gave Andi a sorrowful look. "I really am sorry, Andi." This time he sounded sincere. "I was just foolin' around and didn't think anything would come of it. I reckon I got us all into this fix."

"It's kind of an adventure," Cory said from the other cot. "I've never been in jail before."

"Some adventure," Andi said. For her it was *not* an adventure. It was a disaster. She fell back on the cot and worked on squeezing the water from her two long, dark braids.

Jack joined Cory on the cot. "Deputy Baker is sure taking his time finding a paper and pencil."

"I bet you anything he's taking his time on purpose," Jenny said, "leaving us to sit here and stew. He's a mean one, that deputy."

Just then the door to the sheriff's office opened. Andi and her friends leaped to their feet and shoved their way to the bars. The sooner they gave their names to the deputy, the sooner this whole matter would be done with.

Sure enough, Hugh Baker came through the doorway. But he

had no paper and pencil in his hands. Instead, he was accompanied by an unsmiling Justin Carter. The two men walked up to the cell without speaking.

Andi caught her breath at the sight of her oldest brother. *Oh, no!* She had never seen Justin look so furious. It made her weak with fear. Her throat tightened. *It wasn't my fault!* she wanted to explain. Instead, she backed away from the cell door. Her friends did the same.

Justin gripped the bars of the cell, flicked a quick glance over the prisoners, then turned all his attention on Hugh. "I'd hoped it was merely a vicious rumor begun by some wagging tongues in town," he said in an icy voice. "It's a good thing I decided to check the rumor out. I never considered that you might actually arrest and lock up four minor children without their parents' knowledge."

"I was getting to that, Mr. Carter," Hugh said. "Ten minutes more and the parents would be here, answering to their youngsters' crimes."

"*Crimes?* Don't be ridiculous." Justin laughed. But he didn't look amused.

Hugh crossed his arms and stood his ground. "Don't get on your Carter high horse, Counselor. I'll ask you the same question I asked when you busted into my office two minutes ago. What's your interest here? Surely Sheriff Tate didn't ask a fancy lawyer to watch over his deputy while he's out of town."

Justin ignored Hugh's mocking tone. His voice grew soft and—to Andi's ears—dangerous. She was glad he was talking to the deputy and not to her. "A lot of folks are fed up with the high-handed way you've been doing things since you took this job. Russ needs the help, and that's the only reason you haven't been run out of town on a rail . . . yet. However, when the sheriff gets back from Merced, some of us will be having a word with him about you."

Hugh lost his smug look. "I-I'm just doing my job," he stammered. "I arrest folks. The judge decides if they're guilty or not."

Justin motioned to Hugh's ring of keys. "You've gone too far this time, Deputy Baker. I want my sister and her friends released. You can set whatever fines you think fair for the broken water trough, but that's as far as it goes."

Hugh's eyes flashed. "Your *sister*? So that's what this is all about." He puffed up. "Well, I won't kowtow to you or anybody else when it comes to my job. I locked them up so I could find their folks. Now, unless you got official business here—"

"Deputy! Deputy Baker!" Footsteps clattered through the office. Phil Washburn, the harness maker, poked his head through the open door. "Thank the good Lord I found you. The bank's been robbed. Looks like two—maybe three—gunmen, but nobody knows for sure. There's a dreadful commotion down there. They shot a teller. We need to get a posse together right away."

Hugh's face turned the color of chalk.

"Well, it looks like you've got a *real* crime on your hands now, Deputy," Justin said. He held out his hand for the keys. "I'll take care of this. With any luck, these cells will soon hold a couple of bank robbers instead of kids."

Hugh flung the keys in Justin's direction and raced out the door.

Chapter Three

INTO THE HILLS

A re you sure you're ready for this, Mitch?" Justin leaned over the corral fence and grinned at his sandy-haired younger brother. "After all, you have three jailbirds on your hands for the next couple of weeks. Think you can handle them?"

Andi knew Justin's words were aimed at her. Nobody, but nobody— from the greenest cowhand to her own brothers—would let Andi forget her short stay in Fresno's jail. Even though Justin admitted that this time it wasn't her fault, it didn't stop the teasing that had followed her from morning until night the entire week. She couldn't wait to leave the ranch! Maybe when she and her friends returned from their trek into the mountains, the ranch—and the town—would have forgotten the whole affair.

It didn't help that the *Expositor* had printed the story. Obviously, real news was in short supply these days. It was right there on page three, wedged between an article about a drove of antelope that had crossed the railroad tracks and the news that Charlie Springer, while working on the gate of his irrigation ditch, had inflicted a severe wound on his leg when his axe slipped.

"At least we didn't make the front page," Jenny had said in consolation.

That was true. The front page of the *Expositor* was reserved for the bank robbery, but there hadn't been much to print. The posse had not yet returned with the bank robbers.

Andi looked up from where she was securing her bedroll behind the saddle on Taffy's back. "Justin, do you have to keep bringing that up? I'm tired of your teasing. That's Chad's privilege, not yours."

Justin came around the fence and helped Andi tie up her gear. "Ah, but Chad's been gone all week, chasing after those bank robbers. I thought I'd fill in for him." He winked.

"Don't do him any favors." Andi turned to Jenny and Cory, who were busy with their own gear. "Hurry up, you two! I can't wait to be off."

"Do you want to add anything to Juniper?" Cory asked.

Andi eyed the packhorse Cory had brought along for the trip. The animal was loaded down with more than camping gear. She spied a pickaxe and a couple of shovels sticking out above the rope-wrapped bundles. "Did you put in the gold pan I gave you?"

"Sure did," Cory replied. "I stuffed it in with mine." He scratched behind Juniper's ears and looked at Mitch. "I'm much obliged to you for letting me come along. Pa and Ma say thanks, too. I won't be any trouble. Ma packed me a grub sack, so I've got plenty to eat."

"Glad to have another fellow along," Mitch said. "And we have plenty of food." His blue eyes twinkled in amusement at the sight of Cory's packhorse. "It doesn't look like you have much room for gold, what with all that gear you're packing."

Cory's face reddened. "I like to be prepared."

"I'll say." Mitch chuckled and wandered over to check Jenny's horse.

Fifteen minutes later, they were ready to ride out. The four saddle horses looked eager to be on their way. The two packhorses were loaded down with enough supplies to make camping out for two weeks in the mountains a pleasure rather than an ordeal.

Melinda and their mother wandered out to say good-bye.

"Are you sure you don't want to come along?" Andi asked her sister. She swung her leg over Taffy's back and plunked down in the saddle—her favorite place. "We're going to have a swell time. I brought my fishing pole. When we aren't panning for gold, we'll be fishing. Think of it, Melinda. Fresh trout every night for supper."

"It's tempting," Melinda replied, "but I have other plans."

Andi knew Melinda wasn't really tempted to join them. It was just her polite way of saying, *You won't catch me roughing it for two weeks.*

"Suit yourself," Andi said with a shrug, "but while you're stifling in this heat, helping plan boring Ladies' Aid projects, I'll be riding and fishing and—"

"The Ladies' Aid is a worthy society," Melinda said, narrowing her eyes. "I'll have you know that we—"

"Wear your hats, girls," Elizabeth Carter broke in. "You'll be out in the sun all day, every day. If you're not careful, you'll come home brown as Indians."

This wasn't the first argument Andi's mother had interrupted between her daughters since Andi's return from San Francisco. Melinda seemed to think that two terms at Miss Whitaker's Academy were enough to transform her tomboy little sister into a young lady. Well, Andi had news for her. But she kept her mouth shut, gave Melinda a forced smile, and reached for her hat.

"Maybe Andi'll come home brown," Jenny said from Patches' back, "but I'll come home red as a lobster." She quickly pulled her hat onto her head.

"And Mitchell," Elizabeth added, "go easy on the girls. They're not used to the backcountry."

"Mother!" Andi protested. She didn't know if her mother was teasing or not. "Anywhere Mitch can ride, I can ride. You know that."

Her mother smiled and gave Mitch a look that said, *Look after your sister.*

"Don't worry, Mother." Mitch mounted Chase and took the pack-horse's lead rope from Justin's hand. "Cory and I will keep the girls out of trouble. They'll be too busy to fall off a cliff or drown in the river." He turned to Andi. "You ready to go?"

"You bet!" Andi and Jenny took the lead, leaving Mitch and Cory to bring up the rear with the packhorses. "Good-bye, Mother.

Good-bye, Melinda. 'Bye, Justin," she called as they left the yard and headed for the hills.

They had gone no farther than the main gate when Andi saw a lone man and horse plodding up toward the ranch. It was Chad. He pulled his horse to a stop and waved a tired greeting to the riders. His face showed a week's worth of stubble, and there were dark circles under his eyes. A thick layer of dust clung to his clothes and to his horse.

"You look done in," Mitch said. "Did you catch up with the bank robbers?"

Chad shook his head. He looked too tired to talk, but managed to say, "It was a wasted effort. They got clean away."

"That's too bad. Where did you lose the trail?"

Chad snorted, and a spark of anger flashed in his eyes. "We never *found* the trail. Most of us thought we should split up, but that"—he glanced at the girls—"incompetent, shifty-eyed, greenhorn deputy insisted we stay together. Don't ask me how he decided which way to go. We ended up as far south as the Kings River, then we went around in circles until the rest of us had had enough. By the time the posse figured out we were on a fool's errand, any real trace of the outlaws had disappeared."

Mitch gave a low whistle. "Bet ol' Hugh won't be able to live this one down."

"Sheriff must have been blind and deaf when he hired that young pup," Chad said. "Hugh locks up kids but lets bank robbers get away. That's what *I* call a crime. One good thing did come from all this, though."

"What's that?" Mitch asked.

Chad smiled in satisfaction. "When we dragged ourselves into town this morning, we found the sheriff chomping at the bit, wondering what's been going on. He'd heard about the robbery as soon as he got back to town, but he didn't know where to find us. It drove him nearly loco, having to wait and do nothing." Chad's smile grew wider. "When we told him about the posse's failure, Russ fired Hugh Baker on the spot. And I say good riddance." He gathered his reins and nudged his dusty horse. "I'm hungry and need a bath. Then I plan to sleep for two days straight. You four have a good trip."

The weather had taken a turn for the better, and the morning was cool and fresh. The temperature had dropped at least ten degrees, making it pleasant riding even before they began the climb into the mountains. Andi was convinced that God had brought the cooler weather just to please her and to make the camping trip nearly perfect. Could anything be better than riding Taffy every day, all day, with no chores to interfere with her freedom? Even the river had cooperated with Andi's plans. The San Joaquin was running low—perfect for fording—and Andi and her friends welcomed the excuse to get wet crossing it. She was secretly glad they didn't have to backtrack miles downriver to cross on the ferry.

The sky was so clear and bright with stars that Mitch let everyone stay up late the first night. "You'll be more than ready to hit the hay at sundown about a week from now," he promised. "You might as well enjoy the night sky while you can. We've got a ways to go."

"I'm staying up every night," Andi decided. She stretched out on her bedroll, clasped her hands behind her head, and watched for shooting stars. Above her, the Milky Way spread out across the sky in white splendor.

"Not me." Jenny collapsed on the ground beside Andi and groaned. "I've never been so tuckered out in my life. I'm not used to all this riding." She rubbed her sore backside and yawned. "I feel like I've been riding for two weeks already. I don't think I can keep my eyes open one minute longer—not for all the shooting stars in the sky."

Without even a "good night," Jenny pulled a blanket around her shoulders and turned her back on Andi.

Andi couldn't understand it. She wasn't the least bit tired! The excitement of the first day of her eagerly awaited trip into the mountains had finally arrived, and she wanted to enjoy every minute of it.

"What about you, Cory?" Andi rolled to her side and propped her head up. "Are you going to make a wish on a shooting star?"

Cory sat across from Andi, on the other side of the dying campfire. He was slumped beside an old log, with his head sagging against his chest. At Andi's call, he snapped awake and rubbed his eyes. "Huh? What? Oh, sure. Whatever you say." He grinned.

"You don't even know *what* I said."

Cory's grin turned sheepish. "Hang it all, Andi! Pa roused me out of bed before dawn this morning to do a heap of last-minute chores. He said it was the price of me going along on this trip. I've been trying to stay awake, but it's no use."

A few minutes later, Cory was out cold, sprawled across his bedroll, sleeping the sleep of the dead-tired.

Mitch chuckled. "I guess it's just you and me, sis." He grabbed a rag and lifted the coffeepot from its place over the glowing red embers. Then he poured himself a final cup of the brew and set the pot aside. "Before long it's going to be just you and the stars. I'm about ready to turn in too."

Andi sat up straight and pointed to the sky. "There! I saw the first one."

"So, what's your wish?" Mitch leaned against a log and took a sip of coffee.

Andi felt herself redden. She hadn't expected Mitch to ask her that. Wishes were . . . well . . . private. Mostly private, anyway. But something prodded her to share.

"You won't laugh?"

Mitch shook his head. "Of course I won't."

"I . . . I wish I didn't have to grow up." There. She'd said it. She'd been thinking it ever since she'd returned home from San Francisco, but she hadn't said it out loud. Going to school with twenty other young ladies, learning what was expected when one grew older, and especially seeing the dreadfully boring things young ladies did to occupy their time made her want to scream and run the other way. Then, right on the heels of her return, she'd celebrated her thirteenth birthday. It was downright scary.

Mitch was silent for a moment. He scratched the back of his head, raised the tin cup to his lips, and took another drink. "Why not? It's not so bad."

"That's easy for *you* to say. Or for Chad or Justin." Andi nodded toward the sleeping boy across from them. "Or for Cory. Or any boy. It's different for me." She picked up a small branch and tossed it in the fire. The dying embers sprang to life. "You're doing the same things you did when you were my age. You just grew taller and older and took on more responsibilities. But not Melinda. She used to ride and fish and race with me. Look at her now. She does the dullest things in the world. Sewing circles and quilt-making, or projects that keep her cooped up indoors all day long."

"Maybe she likes doing those things," Mitch suggested.

"Well, *I* don't." Now that her secret wish was out in the open, Andi couldn't stop talking. "I did the right thing the other day at the water trough in town, but I resented it. I wanted to duck my head. Really. I was so hot! But I couldn't. I had to act grown up. I have to do things I don't want to do, and I can't do the things I *want* to do. I want to be outdoors, working with the horses and cattle. I'm good at it—you know I am. Why, I can flush out a stray better than that new cowhand of Chad's. But do you think Chad will let me? Oh, no! He'd rather put up with Ralph's fumbling then let me help. I bet if we were dirt-poor ranchers he'd be mighty glad of my help." She sighed. "Girls can't be cowboys. You know it. I know it. And mostly . . . Mother knows it."

Andi could see Mitch's lips twitching in the red glow of the camp-fire. "You promised not to laugh."

"I wasn't laughing," Mitch replied. "I was thinking. I've heard tell of a girl back east . . . what is her name? Annie something." He snapped his fingers. "That's it. Annie Oakley. Just a slip of a girl, not much older than Melinda. She does something no one ever thought a girl should do. She shoots. She travels around the country trick shooting. I reckon a lot of folks told her she couldn't do that. It's not 'proper' for a young lady to shoot guns"—he grinned—"especially if she can outshoot the men. But she pays 'em no mind and goes ahead and does what she's good at."

Andi's eyes opened wide, and she gaped at her brother. "Really? You're not teasing me or trying to make me feel better?"

"No, sirree. It's true. I read about it the other day. Just a few lines in the *Expositor*, but it grabbed my attention. If Annie Oakley's as good as they say, I reckon we'll be hearing a lot more about her in the next few years." He glanced into his tin cup then tossed the remains of his coffee onto the coals, where it sizzled. "I don't know if Mother has mentioned this to you, but growing up has more to do with putting aside childish behavior and facing new responsibilities than turning into some kind of proper lady with fine airs."

"She might have brought it up a time or two," Andi admitted. *Like once a week since I got home,* she added to herself.

"Well, personally, I'd rather have a sensible young woman around— one who can think clearly and do what's got to be done—than an addle-headed 'lady' whose head is filled with nothing but the latest fashions and how to catch a beau." He reached out and caught Andi's hand. "If you concentrate on being the first example, I think you'll find out that growing up isn't so bad, after all." He gave her hand a squeeze and let go. "It's late, and we've got a long ride ahead of us. We really have to turn in."

Andi nodded. It had worked out well that her friends had fallen asleep. How often did she get a chance to sit and talk with Mitch? She was suddenly glad she'd shared her shooting star wish with him. *Annie Oakley, huh? I'm going to have to find out more about that young woman.* She glanced up at the star-washed sky and said, "I've thought of a better wish to go along with that shooting star I saw earlier."

"Yeah?"

"I hope these two weeks last a long, long time. I've never enjoyed myself more."

"You know what, Andi?" Mitch replied. "Neither have I."

Chapter Four

GOLD FEVER

Andi heard the creek before she saw it. It splashed and tumbled far below the narrow trail they'd been following all morning—a little-used path, no wider than the packs on Juniper's back. It twisted and turned between pine trees, scrub oak, and manzanita, gradually climbing higher and higher into the mountains. How Mitch had found this trail was more than Andi could figure out. To her, it was nothing more than a tiny thread that weaved its way through a vast, tree-filled country that seemed to stretch on forever, always upward, toward the towering peaks of the Sierra Nevada.

Andi had never thought about how easily one could get lost in such a wilderness. The Circle C ranch spread out over thousands of acres, but she knew the ranch like the back of her hand, or at least most of it. True, it was incredibly easy to get turned around in the low-lying hills. They really did all look alike. But as long as the sun was shining, Andi could find her way home.

Here in the heart of the Sierras, the word *lost* took on new meaning. Steep, rock-encrusted gullies, ridges that went on for miles, and dark pine and sequoia forests marked this place as dangerous to the inexperienced traveler. Andi, for one, did not want to be left on her own in these mountains.

"Do you hear the creek?" she called to Mitch, who waved a hand to indicate that he had.

It was Andi's turn to keep a grip on the Carter packhorse, Pepper, so she and Cory, with Juniper, lagged behind Mitch and Jenny. The trail cut across the face of yet another ridge, forcing the riders to go along single-file. It was slow going, but Mitch didn't appear to be in a hurry. Andi wondered if this trail was a taste of what the rest of the trip up to the logging camp would be like. Two weeks suddenly didn't seem like near enough time to reach the camp, conduct whatever business Mitch needed to conduct, and get back to the ranch.

But then, this was only the middle of the third day.

Andi glanced back at Cory. He was trying to keep a firm grip on Juniper and read his survey map at the same time. He'd wrapped Flash's reins around his saddle horn and given the gelding his head. Now Cory had a free hand to hold the map steady while he studied it.

Andi shook her head. It was a wonder Cory hadn't gone over the edge. He looked just as at ease riding a hair's breadth away from a hundred-foot drop as if he were riding down the main street of Fresno. Andi wished she felt as calm.

"I think this is a likely creek," Cory said without looking up. "According to the place Mitch marked, where we camped last night, this here should be Gold Creek." He glanced up. "There are pickaxe symbols on the map. They wouldn't have named it Gold Creek if there wasn't any gold in it."

"Sure they would have," Andi replied over her shoulder. "They might've named it that with the *hope* there was gold in it."

Cory gave her a sour look and returned to studying his map. "If this creek doesn't work out, we can try Alder or Pine creeks. They're in the general direction of the logging camp . . . or maybe your brother will give in and let us try our luck in an old mine. Looks like there's plenty of those around here. But they're up on the ridges. You think he might?"

Andi shook her head and carefully eased Taffy around a large rock jutting up through the trail. "Not a chance. Old, abandoned mines are dangerous . . . and dark," she said with a shudder. She much preferred to look for gold out in the open, exploring a friendly creek.

If she didn't find any gold, a fish would work just as well right about now. Her stomach rumbled.

It was too much trouble to keep turning around to talk to Cory, so Andi focused on the trail ahead of her and on Jenny's plaid back. She couldn't help smiling at Jenny's response from the week before, when a pair of Mitch's outgrown trousers had been cut off and held up around her middle by a set of suspenders. "This is more like it!" Jenny had crowed. "I feel right at home now." With her plaid shirt, Jenny looked like a small logger sitting on Patches. All she lacked was a double-bit axe.

The trail took a sudden downturn. Slowly, Mitch led the riders the length of a steep, rocky slope that opened up alongside a bubbling creek. The horses wasted no time helping themselves to a long, cold drink.

Andi slid from Taffy's back with a groan of relief. She'd been riding since dawn, and the sun was now high overhead. She tore off her hat, boots, and socks and plunged into the creek alongside her horse. "Oh, it's cold!" she yelled gleefully. She reached down and drank her fill of the clear water. When she looked up, a double handful of water smacked her in the face.

For once, neither Andi nor Jenny had to worry that someone would spoil their fun. The creek was shallow in places, but wide. They found a spot where the water had cut a deep pool in the rock along the far bank and pelted each other and Cory with water. To Andi's surprise and delight, Mitch joined them. It wasn't long before everyone was soaked to the skin, refreshingly cool, and hungry.

"That's enough horsing around for now," Mitch said as he dragged himself from the stream. He lay against the rocks, breathing hard. Water dripped from his dark blond hair into his eyes. "You three win. Let's set up camp and get something to eat. Then"—he looked at Cory—"you can start panning for that treasure you're so fired up about."

"Yes, *sir!*" Cory scrambled from the water. He looked eager to help Mitch set up camp. There were plenty of good, sandy camping spots where the creek bank widened, away from the rocks and out from under the sizzling mountain sun. It took no time at all to unsaddle the horses and hobble them in a small, grassy meadow. Andi and Jenny unloaded Pepper's packs and set him to graze with the other horses. Cory did the same with Juniper, and soon the camp was ready.

They ate the last of the picnic lunch Elizabeth had sent along with them two days before. From now on, if they didn't catch or shoot their meals, they'd be stuck eating beans and jerky, along with a few pan biscuits, which didn't suit Andi at all.

They had traveled hard the past two and a half days, so it felt good to take an entire afternoon to sit and enjoy the mountains, the creek, and the trees. But Cory would have none of it. They had no sooner cleared away the remains of their meal when he started unpacking his bundles. With a clatter, Cory scattered gold pans and shovels and pickaxes on the ground.

Mitch looked up from where he was leaning against a tall pine, untangling his fishing line. "Take it easy, Cory. The gold's not running away. Can't a man have an hour of peace and quiet without all that racket?" He shook his head, gathered up his pole and bait, and meandered his way upstream. "Good luck with your gold panning. I'm off to catch us some supper."

As soon as Mitch was out of sight round the bend, Andi, Cory, and Jenny snatched up their pans. Cory grabbed a shovel and they set out to find the perfect spot to pan for gold.

"Everybody spread out," Cory instructed. "That way nobody's stirring up the water for anybody else."

Jenny looked at her gold pan with a critical eye. "So, what happens? You dip the pan in the creek, and the gold flows right in?"

Andi and Cory looked at each other. Cory grinned. "Not exactly."

"Haven't you ever panned for gold?" Andi asked.

Jenny shrugged. "Can't say that I have. There's no gold where I come from—leastways, I haven't heard of any. There's coal, of course. Up in the hills. Lots of it. But they don't mine it with this kind of pan." She held it up. "This looks more like a tin plate for eating than for finding gold."

"You go on, Cory," Andi said. "I'll show Jenny how it's done." She grabbed Jenny's hand. "Come on." Together, they waded across the creek, away from Cory's "claim." Andi saw Mitch upstream, above a small waterfall, lying in the shade with his fishing pole in the water. He looked asleep.

"What are you looking for?" Jenny asked a few minutes later as they wandered up and down the creek bank.

"I'm looking for a nice, quiet bend in the creek where gold might have washed up—a spot that's full of sand and gravel. Gold is heavier than other minerals. It stays in the pan when the dirt and rocks wash downstream. You'll see. Here's a good place. Watch me."

Andi squatted by the creek bank and dipped her pan in the shallow, still water. When she lifted it up, a mixture of small gravel, sand, and water filled the pan. "Now the tricky part," she told Jenny. "You've got to wash the gravel and sand back into the creek, dip up more water, wash again, and keep going until there's nothing left but a little fine silt, along with—we hope—some flakes of gold. Or if we're lucky, a nugget. But I'm not counting too much on that. You have to be very, very careful. If you swish the water too fast, the tiny pieces of gold slide right out of the pan and back into the creek."

Andi began to slosh the gravel and water around in the pan. The large chunks tumbled out first, followed later by smaller rocks and sand. She continued to add water, swirl, and watch as more sand and gravel slid into the creek, again and again.

"You're joking."

Andi looked up from her pan. Her friend stood knee-deep in the creek, her hand dangling limply at her side, clutching the pan. Dark red tangles plastered her face and shoulders. She was not smiling. "No, I'm serious," Andi said. "That's the way it's done. It takes a lot of patience."

Jenny let out a long breath and crouched next to Andi to watch. She didn't look excited about the idea of panning for gold.

Andi squinted into her dark pan. Along one edge, a flake of something shiny glinted up at her. It was about half the size of her little fingernail. She saw more specks, no bigger than pinheads. "Look here, Jenny," she said, pointing to the yellow particles. "It's gold."

Jenny looked a bit more interested. She peered into the pan to see what Andi had found. "Mighty tiny, if you ask me," she said with a snort. "Why, at the rate you're going, it would take days and days to pan enough gold to buy a decent meal."

Andi reached into her pocket and pulled out a small pair of tweezers she'd brought along. Carefully, she lifted the tiny flake from the silt and thrust the gold pan at Jenny. "Here, hold this." She reached into another pocket and brought out a small glass medicine vial. "Why do you think nobody bothers with these diggings anymore? It's mostly played out. Some gold still trickles down from the mountains, but not enough to get excited about. Panning for gold takes a long time. I was lucky to see color right off. Sometimes you swirl and wash and find nothing. Then you have to start all over again."

She pulled the cork lid from the vial and dropped the gold flake in. "There. My first flake. Shall we try it again?"

Jenny shrugged and lifted her pan. "I'm game if you are."

Andi, Jenny, and Cory spent the rest of the afternoon sloshing around in the creek, panning for gold. As determined as Jenny appeared to master the skill of swirling her pan, she never quite got the hang of it. Sand and gravel flew everywhere, along with water and—most likely—any gold that might have been in the pan. Once, in a fit, Jenny pitched her gold pan clear across the creek.

"What fool would spend all his time squatting in a freezing cold creek and playing in the dirt for a few pieces of gold?" she hollered.

Andi laughed. "You'd better fetch your pan before it gets loose from those rocks and floats away downstream." But secretly she was thinking the same thing. For all her long hours of work, she had one nugget the size of a wheat kernel and two nice-sized gold flakes, along with the tiny flake from her first pan. She was hot, wet, hungry, and tired. The sun was quickly falling behind the trees, and it wouldn't be long before the chilly mountain evening set in. If she didn't dry off before dusk, she'd be shivering with cold tonight.

Andi pulled herself up from her special "claim" and gathered her pan. Across the creek, Mitch was waving and holding up a stringer full of trout. Andi's mouth watered at the sight. She would have traded her entire vial of gold flakes for one fish. *No wonder all those shopkeepers made a fortune during the gold rush,* she thought. *A hungry gold miner would pay 'most anything for a meal or a drink.* Her stomach cried out for something to eat.

She waded through the bubbling water, with Jenny a few paces behind, and climbed out near their campsite.

Cory met them with a wide smile. "Look here, Andi. It won't take any time at all to pan an ounce of gold at this rate." He handed her a small vial, where three small nuggets bounced around as she shook it. A couple of small flakes were mixed in with the nuggets. Andi peered closely at Cory's "treasure." It didn't look anything like the thumb-sized amount of gold needed to make an ounce. But Cory appeared to have had a swell time panning for gold.

She handed back his vial and held up her own. "You have a nice start. Here's mine."

Cory admired it, then looked up. "How 'bout you, Jenny? Find any color?"

"Nope. Don't care, either. Panning for gold is nothing but hard work. No fun at all."

"Don't worry," Cory assured her. "The deal was that we split whatever we find three ways. I'll keep my end of the bargain, even if you never find any gold."

Jenny's mouth dropped open, and she looked at Cory with respect. "That's mighty generous of you, Cory. Thanks."

There was no more time to share gold stories. Mitch put them to work cleaning the fish, while he started the fire and pulled out the frying pans. Along with the trout, he sliced up a few potatoes, sprinkled them liberally with salt and pepper, and put everything over the now-hot campfire. The smell of frying fish and potatoes rose and filled the campsite until Andi couldn't bear it one minute longer. She reached over the fire and nearly singed the ends of her braids when she fished out a piece of potato to sample. The reward for her impatience was a couple of scorched fingers and a burnt tongue.

"Serves you right," Mitch said as she ran to the creek to soak her fingers in the cold water.

Andi planned to stay up that night and watch for shooting stars, but she couldn't keep her eyes open. It seemed like only a minute passed before Mitch was rousing her. "We've got a lot of miles to cover today. Get up. Let's go."

Yawning, Andi and Jenny stumbled to the creek to wash up. The water was icy cold. The tall pines, which yesterday had offered shady relief from the sun, blocked the few warming rays that peeked over the mountains. Andi shivered in her still-damp clothes.

They ate a quick breakfast and hurried to pack up camp. Jenny ran to unhobble the horses. "I want a head start saddling Patches," she called over her shoulder, "so nobody will have to wait for me today."

Andi worked a few minutes before joining Jenny. She secured her gold pan on Juniper and began rolling up her bedding. Then she paused. A strange buzzing noise near the horses made her prick up her ears. She glanced at Jenny, who was wrestling with Patches' saddle, unaware of the sound.

The buzzing turned more insistent, and Patches reared. The finger of worry that had tickled Andi's mind suddenly clutched her throat and turned it dry. She knew that sound.

It was a rattlesnake.

Chapter Five

CHANGE OF PLANS

Andi sprang to her feet. The saddle hung lopsided—half on, half off Patches. Jenny was trying desperately to steady the heavy piece of tack.

"Jenny! Forget the saddle. Get away from the horse!" Andi shouted.

Too late. The pinto reared again, nostrils flaring. Then he pivoted, sending the saddle flying through the air. One flailing hoof grazed Jenny's shoulder, and she dropped to the ground with a sharp cry. But instead of scuttling away from the rearing horse, she lay still, only a few feet from Patches' hooves.

Andi gasped and dashed toward her friend, heedless of the snake. *Oh, please, God, don't let Jenny be hurt bad!* She prayed on the run and reached Jenny and Patches in seconds. But before she could fall at her friend's side, Mitch came up from behind and yanked her away.

"Stay back!" he barked. He turned to Cory. "Get my gun. It's in the saddlebag."

Cory took off like a shot while Andi stared at the huge rattlesnake under Patches' hooves. The pinto reared up one final time and came down in the middle of the creature's thick, writhing body. Then Patches shook his mane, snorted, and moved off.

"Here," Cory panted and handed Mitch the gun. But it looked like Patches had done a thorough job of killing the snake.

"Stay where you are until I make sure the snake is dead," Mitch said.

"But Jenny needs—"

"She'll keep." Mitch picked up a long stick and cautiously made his way to the half-coiled body on the ground. He poked it once, twice, but nothing happened. "It's dead. Go see to Jenny, but give that snake a wide berth."

Andi didn't care anything about the snake. She rushed to Jenny's side, heart pounding, and fell to the ground beside her. Tears welled up at the sight of her friend's pale face and closed eyes. "Mitch, come quick! Do you think the snake bit her?"

"I don't think so," Mitch said, kneeling next to the girls. "Patches was too quick. But I saw him catch her on the shoulder. She's going to be hurting when she wakes up."

Andi sniffed back her tears. "If she dies out here, it will be my fault. Going along with you on this camping trip was my idea."

"Jenny's not going to die," Mitch said. "Leastways, not any time soon. She probably knocked herself out when she hit the ground. Look, she's coming around."

Sure enough, Jenny's eyes opened. "W-what happened?" she mumbled. She tried sitting up, but fell back with a groan. "Oh, my head hurts! And my shoulder." She moaned.

"Don't try to get up," Mitch ordered. He sent Cory for a pan of water and some rags, then turned back to Jenny. "It looks like you put a gash in the back of your head when Patches knocked you down. Do you remember anything?"

"Did the snake strike out at you?" Andi burst out in a half-sob.

"Andi, don't scare her," Mitch said.

Jenny's brown eyes widened. She lay on her back and looked first at Andi and then at Mitch. "Snake? What snake? All I remember is the horse rearing up for no reason. Thought maybe he didn't want the saddle on his back. He started dancing around . . ." She gasped. "I *do* remember hearing a funny sound—a kind of buzzing coming from the ground. But I had no time to figure out what it was. Patches just started rearing." She frowned and brought her hand up to her left shoulder. She winced. "I guess I got in his way."

"It was a rattlesnake," Andi said with a shudder. She looked around, wondering where the creature had come from. There were plenty of rocks and crannies nearby. No doubt the snake had emerged from its hiding place, hoping to catch a little morning sun and warm up. She brushed a sleeve across her wet face and took a deep, calming breath. "I've never been so scared in my life. I thought you'd been bit. I thought . . ." She couldn't go on. Her heart was slowly returning to normal, but the knot in her stomach hadn't yet unwound.

"Here's the water," Cory said from behind. He handed over a pan and the clean rags. "Mind if I keep the snake, Mitch?" Slung over his shoulder was an empty burlap sack. "I'll turn it in for the bounty when we get back."

Mitch shrugged. "Suit yourself. I've got no use for it, unless"—he winked at Jenny—"this young lady would like to enjoy a tasty rattle-snake meal at our next camp site."

Jenny gasped. "You're joshin' me, right? Nobody eats . . . snake." She shuddered.

"We do," Andi and Cory said together.

"It's actually not too bad," Cory went on. "Sort of tastes like . . ." He paused.

"Chicken," Andi finished for him. "I've only had it once or twice, but it beats eating jerky by a long shot." She made a face. "I hate jerky."

"We'll even give you the rattle as a memento of your stay in the Sierras," Cory added generously.

Jenny gave Cory a tiny smile. "That sure would be something to show my brothers when I get home. We don't have rattlesnakes in Tacoma, or any other pesky, dangerous crawly critters, for that matter. Maybe it's too cold and wet for them."

While Cory ran off to collect their future evening meal, Andi helped Jenny sit up so Mitch could take a closer look at her shoulder and head.

"Can you move your left arm?" he asked.

Jenny nodded and raised her arm above her head. Then she lowered it and winced. "It hurts something fierce. I bet I end up with a bruise the size of Patches' hoof. But it won't interfere with my riding," she added quickly. She and Andi exchanged worried looks. Would Mitch turn around and take everyone home over one little accident?

"Hmm," Mitch said. He was busy examining the back of Jenny's head. "This might hurt a bit." He dipped the rag into the pan of water and began to wash away the blood. Jenny yelped. "Sorry," Mitch said, but he continued to wipe the wound clean.

Andi stared at a lump the size of a small plum, which showed a deep gash right down the middle. Blood flowed freely from the cut, a dark stain against Jenny's bright red hair. "That doesn't look so good," she remarked. Then, "Oops. Sorry, Jenny."

Mitch agreed. He wrapped a clean rag around her head and tied the ends. "This will help slow the bleeding, but I think a doctor better take a look at it. You might need stitches."

"Oh, no, I don't," Jenny insisted with a scowl. "Nobody's gonna sew me up like a piece of cloth. My brother Eli cut his arm real bad a few years ago. Logging accident. They doused his arm with whiskey, and my mama sewed him up. The doc was out of town." She shuddered. "Eli's a grown man, and he hollered plenty. Told me it hurt worse getting sewed up than being cut in the first place."

Andi cringed at Jenny's story. No wonder her friend didn't want to see the doctor. But there had to be a way to convince Jenny to go along with it. "I got stitches once. See?" Andi pulled the hair away from the left side of her head. Even now, nearly a year later, the scar still showed. "It's a gunshot wound. It didn't hurt at all when Doc Weaver stitched it up."

Jenny looked unconvinced. "Probably because you were unconscious."

Mitch chuckled. "You got that right. She was out cold."

"I was trying to make it easier on you," Andi said with a deep sigh. "At least let a doctor look at it."

"I'm fine," Jenny insisted. "I don't need any doctor poking and prodding me."

Mitch rose, holding the pan and the rags. "It's not open for discussion. We're going down to Fresno Flats. It's a little mountain town not too far from here. We'll easily make it before noon. After the doc tends to Jenny, *I'll* decide what we do next."

Mitch's words cast a gloom over the small group. Andi sighed and helped Jenny stand up.

Jenny took a couple of cautious steps and announced, "See? I'm fine." But the tight grip on her arm told Andi that her friend was hurting.

"What if the doctor doesn't think Jenny should keep going?" Cory asked from Jenny's other side. He reached out to lend a hand, but she brushed his help away.

"We'll cross that bridge when we come to it," Mitch said. He dumped the water, wrung out the rags, and began to stow everything back on the packhorse. "Jenny," he ordered without turning around, "you ride with Andi. I don't want you tumbling off your horse in a dead faint an hour from now."

Jenny opened her mouth to protest, but Andi yanked her toward Taffy. "Don't argue," she quietly warned her friend. "Mitch is real easygoing most times, but if he sets his mind on something, he can be as hard-headed as Chad." She mounted Taffy and reached out to give Jenny a hand up behind her.

Jenny lifted her good arm to Andi, but she swayed and nearly fell over when she tried to put her foot in the stirrup. Andi held her hand tightly and waited for the weak moment to pass. "If Mitch saw you ready to keel over like that, our camping trip would be over," she said when Jenny finally pulled herself up behind Andi. "Lucky for you, he was helping Cory pack up the rest of the gear."

"Will your brother really haul us back to the ranch?" Jenny whispered.

"I don't know. If it were Cory or me who was hurt, Mitch *might* be willing to take it easy for the rest of the day and see what happens." She shrugged. "You're a guest. I don't think he wants to take any chances."

Jenny snorted. "I've fallen out of tall trees and hit my head dozens of times. I tell you, I'm fine. I don't want to go back."

Andi didn't want to go back, either. But there was no use pleading with Mitch. This was one of those times when sweet-talking definitely would not work.

It was a somber little group that wound its way along the trail. Nobody felt much like talking. To Andi, it looked like they were following the same trail they'd taken the day before. Only this time they were going the wrong way.

Chapter Six

FRESNO FLATS

They rode into Fresno Flats just before noon. It was a pleasant-looking town, surrounded by mountains. One main road cut the small village in two. A couple of saloons, a hotel and restaurant, a livery and stage stop, as well as a Chinese laundry and a post office lined the street. A generous number of oaks and pines provided shade and gave the town a certain charm in spite of the dust and heat.

A small group of children paused and looked up from their play as the four travelers plodded down the street and pulled their horses to a stop in front of the post office. Mitch dismounted. "There's no sheriff's office, so I'll check with the postmaster to see where the doctor lives."

"If there *is* a doctor," Cory muttered, flicking his gaze around the tiny town.

Before Andi could comment, Mitch was back. He pulled off his hat, wiped away the sweat, and plopped it back on his head. "I guess Fresno Flats has mail service every other week, and this is the off week. The postmaster is out." He motioned to Cory. "Come along with me. If we split up, we'll surely find somebody who can point the way to a doctor."

"What about Jenny and me?" Andi wanted to know. Going from the mountains to the lower elevation of the Flats reminded her of how hot it was today. She didn't feel like sitting on her horse while Mitch and Cory ambled around town looking for a doctor.

Mitch squinted against the bright noon sun. "Dismount and stay put 'til Cory and I get back."

Andi slipped to the ground beside Taffy. She reached up to steady Jenny while she dismounted. Her friend looked ready to faint. Andi hoped Jenny's shakiness was from too much sun and not the result of her wound. She gave the back of Jenny's head a quick glance and bit her lip. A considerable amount of blood had soaked through the makeshift bandage. *This is not good,* Andi thought, but she said nothing to Jenny.

Together they found a comfortable spot under the wide, spreading branches of an oak tree and waited. And waited. The minutes ticked by, but Cory and Mitch did not return. Andi leaned back against the tree trunk, closed her eyes, and worried. Would Mitch find a doctor? Would he make them stay in town until he was satisfied that Jenny was on the mend? Worse, would he leave them behind at the hotel and finish the trip to the logging camp alone? What a terrible thought! Andi's heart thumped as her imagination took off. *Oh, why does Mitch have to be so cautious?*

An elbow in her side roused Andi from her dreary thoughts. "Andi!" Jenny's voice was a harsh whisper in her ear.

She startled and opened her eyes. "What? Is Mitch back?"

Jenny shook her head. "No, but I think I see . . ." She paused and pointed across the street at the saloon.

"So? It's a saloon. I'm sure Mitch didn't take Cory in there."

"No, Andi. You might think I'm crazy, but I saw somebody we know go into the saloon."

Andi sat up straight and brushed her mental cobwebs away. "Who do we know in this town?"

Jenny snorted. "Nobody but that greenhorn deputy who locked us up a couple weeks back. Do you suppose he's hunting a new job?"

Andi considered. It seemed reasonable that Hugh Baker would be looking for another job. He'd been fired less than a week ago. Why not try for a position in Fresno Flats? Then she shrugged and fell back against the tree. "Who cares? The farther away from *our* Fresno he stays, the happier I'll be. I never want to run into that deputy again. Besides, how do you know it's him?"

"He's short and skinny, and has a certain way of strutting that caught my attention," Jenny said with a glint in her eye. "Your brother said this town hasn't any sheriff, so Hugh might be trying to get hired." She frowned. "Maybe we should warn the townsfolk not to hire him."

"Maybe we should mind our own business," Andi said. "I'd just as soon stay out of his way." A new thought crossed her mind. "Maybe he's already been hired."

Jenny clutched Andi's arm. "Look! That's him, isn't it?" She pointed at the saloon, where a short, bow-legged young man in a blue shirt and dark vest was leaving the building. Even from across the street Andi recognized Hugh Baker's confident swagger and slight build.

In a flash, Andi was on her feet. She scrambled around the tree and peeked out from behind its thick trunk. "Yep, that's him." She scowled when Jenny burst into laughter. "Laugh all you want, Jenny Grant, but I don't trust Deputy—I mean *former* Deputy Baker. He didn't like the idea that Justin was bailing us out of jail. No, sirree. What if he really is the new sheriff here? If he sees us, he might find a reason to arrest us out of spite—for loitering or something—and Justin's nowhere around. We need to lie low until we're out of this town."

Jenny's laughter died. She joined Andi behind the tree. Together they watched Hugh cross the street and saunter down the road toward the hotel and restaurant. He appeared perfectly at ease, as if Fresno Flats were "his" town.

Just then a stagecoach, pulled by four horses, rolled into town and pulled to a stop in front of the hotel. When the dust settled, half a dozen smartly dressed men and women stepped down from the stage and disappeared into the restaurant.

Jenny whistled. "What's a passel of highfalutin ladies and gentlemen doing *here*? Surely they didn't come all the way up to this little village to eat lunch."

"It's the Madera stage to Yosemite," Mitch offered from behind the girls. They whirled. "Fresno Flats is the noon dinner stop. All sorts of folks go up to Yosemite for a look-see. A couple of years ago General Grant and his family took the trip. Don't you remember, Andi, when all those folks from Fresno went up to Madera to gawk at the general?" He pushed his hat back and grinned. "A more interesting question is . . . why are you two hiding behind a tree?"

Andi didn't want to admit that she was hiding from Hugh Baker, but Jenny spilled the story with pleasure. Instead of laughing as Andi expected, Cory gaped, and his look turned worried.

"Where is he now?" he asked.

"We saw him go in the hotel," Jenny said, "but we haven't seen him come out."

Mitch waved it off. "Let's not waste our time worrying about that deputy. What's more important is that this town doesn't have a resident doctor."

Andi's heart sank.

"Yep," Cory put in, "the closest thing to a doctor is the livery-stable owner, who doctors the horses. He's stitched up a fair number of cuts and said he'd take a look at your head."

Jenny's face turned white. "A horse doctor?"

Cory burst into laughter. "It's true, Jenny. He told me so himself."

"Lucky for you," Mitch broke in, "I talked with a woman who was a nurse during the War Between the States. She's an older lady, the wife of the minister. She's happy to dress your wound and stitch it up, if necessary."

Andi giggled, relieved there was someone who could care for her friend. "Are you going to take Cory's offer or Mitch's?"

"Actually," Jenny said, "I'm feeling right as rain. My rest in the shade has revived me considerably. But," she added quickly at Mitch's frown, "if I have to choose, I'll take the nurse-lady."

"So, you're heading up to Sugar Pine Camp, are you?" Mrs. Simmons didn't wait for an answer. Her tongue was as efficient at prattling as her fingers were at examining hurt people. She probed Jenny's head wound with a gentle touch, uttered a "tsk-tsk," and continued talking to her captive audience. "I was mighty glad when the Madera Flume Company took over the lumbering up there after them other folks went bust. We thought this town would shrivel up and die back in '78." She shuddered at old memories and dabbed a generous glob of iodine-soaked cotton on Jenny's cut.

Jenny yelped and sprang from her seat. "That hurts!"

"Steady now, honey." Mrs. Simmons gave Jenny an understanding smile. "That's all the pain I'll be giving you today." She laid her plump, snow-white hands on Jenny's shoulders and guided her into the straight-back chair. "You won't be needing stitches, after all. Head wounds bleed worse than a stuck pig, but the bleeding's slowed down now. I'll apply a poultice to draw out any infection, and I'll wrap your head up tight." She clucked her tongue. "You'll have a fine bruise in a day or two from that kick to your shoulder, but nothing permanent. You'll be good as new in a few days."

"I've got to go around with an ol' bandage wrapped around my head?" Jenny burst out in dismay.

Andi hid a smile behind her hand. Jenny looked as helpless as a trussed-up calf. Although there were no ropes tying Jenny to the chair, this heavy woman with twinkling brown eyes and dimples in her round cheeks held her patient captive by her very presence. Any woman who was used to nursing hardened soldiers on a battlefield could keep Jenny in line, Andi figured. She glanced at her brother and Cory, sitting across the kitchen table from her. Mrs. Simmons was holding them all captive with her constant chatter. Andi cupped her chin in her hands and rested her elbows on the table, resigned.

"That's quite a sawmill operation they got going up at the camp," Mrs. Simmons continued. Her hands fluttered as she arranged the bandage. "And that flume! It's the beatin'est thing I ever did see. Sixty miles—all the way down to Madera from the camp. It's a wonder, it is. You going to work for them? You don't look like a logger or a sawyer to me." She held Mitch's gaze and waited for his answer.

Mitch gave her a charming smile. "Not quite, ma'am. My family is part owner in the new company, and I was elected to go up and get acquainted."

"Oh, that's grand! Real nice of you to take a personal interest in your family's holdings." The jolly woman tied Jenny's bandage and snipped off the extra lengths of white cloth with a pair of shears. Then she whipped out a small mirror and shoved it in Jenny's face. "There you go, honey. What do you think?"

Jenny peered at herself in the hand mirror. "Thank you, ma'am."

"So, you say you're from Fresno?" Mrs. Simmons began collecting the discarded rags and pans and medicines.

"Yes, ma'am," Mitch said.

"You'd have been better off taking the train to Madera and coming up on the stage. Safer for the youngsters too. You could have avoided those dangerous mountain trails. Twisting and turning up and down, only the good Lord knows where. It's a wonder you haven't gone over the edge and found yourselves at the bottom of a draw." She clucked her tongue.

Andi simmered. Mrs. Simmons had no right to criticize her brother. "Mitch knows how to travel in the backcountry," she said.

Mitch silenced Andi with a look. "We've been taking our time, doing a little gold panning along the way."

Mrs. Simmons brightened. "You don't say! Have you heard about the strike up on Potter's Ridge?" Without waiting for an answer, she said, "That's an added boost to business in this town. Things are looking up around here. They surely are." Then she frowned. "I s'pose you'll head back up the trail rather than do the sensible thing and take the main road to the logging camp?"

Andi held her breath. *Say yes, Mitch.*

"So long as Jenny is up to the trip."

Mrs. Simmons waved away Mitch's concern. "She's right as rain. It wasn't near as bad as it looked once all the blood was cleared away. If you're dead set on taking the trails, at least stay in a cabin when you can. You're bound to come across one or two abandoned ones." She eyed Jenny. "Wouldn't hurt to keep her off the hard ground." Then as quickly as the passing of a summer storm she smiled and said, "You'll stay for tea, of course."

As soon as the invitation to tea rolled off Mrs. Simmons's tongue, Andi knew they would be corralled here for a good part of the afternoon. After all, they were obliged to her for seeing to Jenny. When Mrs. Simmons turned to put the kettle on, Andi leaned across the table and whispered, "When can we leave? It's getting late."

Mitch frowned and shook his head.

Andi slumped. How much longer would they be stuck here?

Chapter Seven

THE SHACK

O uch! How dare you take a nip at me!" Andi whacked the pack-horse on the neck. "You don't have much to carry, while Taffy and the other horses have to haul all of us around." Pepper laid his ears back and stamped a hoof on the ground. His sour mood reflected Andi's like a mirror.

A whole day wasted! She dared not say anything aloud, but she knew Cory and Jenny were feeling restless and impatient as well. The three of them had fidgeted most of the afternoon yesterday while Mitch and Mrs. Simmons chatted. "Correction," Andi grumbled as she tied down the bundles on Pepper's back, "Mrs. Simmons talked. Mitch listened."

They'd learned more than they ever wanted to know about the founding of Fresno Flats, the new gold strike up on the ridge, and the dangers of getting lost in the mountains. "Why, just last year, Joey Butterfield wandered off from the school picnic out at the Morton ranch," Mrs. Simmons lamented. "They found him two days later at the bottom of a draw. Had a broken leg that never did heal proper. Limps to this day." She let out a mournful sigh. "And this spring, a mountain lion . . ." On and on she prattled.

If it hadn't been for the timely arrival of the Reverend Simmons, they would certainly have been forced to spend the night in town. To Andi's relief, the minister asked his wife to accompany him to an outlying ranch. Mrs. Simmons had quickly tied up a bundle of food for their supper and had sent them on their way with a hearty, "I so enjoyed your company. Do stop by for another visit sometime."

Andi snapped back to the present at Mitch's cheery, "Let's go, Andi." He seemed in good spirits this morning in spite of the fact that they'd traveled only a few miles out of town before having to set up camp for the night.

Nothing ever riles him much, Andi thought. She, on the other hand, was plenty riled. She choked back her grumblings and secured the final knot in Pepper's packs. "I'm ready." She pasted a smile on her face.

"We'll have to make up time today, or we'll arrive at the camp only to turn around and head home." He reached out his hand. "Toss me the line and I'll deal with Pepper. He's acting cranky."

Andi handed Mitch the lead rope and mounted Taffy, who seemed as willing as her mistress to be off. "You got tired of standing around in town all afternoon too, I bet," she whispered to the mare.

The morning passed in wonder and delight as the travelers climbed higher and higher into the mountains. Andi's grumpiness over the wasted afternoon melted away when she took in the beauty of the forest, the bright blue sky, and the vastness of the wilderness. She looked at Jenny and was suddenly ashamed that she'd thought yesterday dreadfully long and dull. *I'm sorry, Lord,* she prayed. *I forgot why we went to town in the first place. Thank you for mending Jenny.*

Andi's heart felt lighter after her prayer. She determined to stay focused on the good things about this trip—riding, fishing, panning for gold, and being together.

Mitch kept them at a steady pace, stopping only to water the horses when the trail crossed an occasional rocky creek. The heat of the early summer did not touch the travelers, for a cool breeze blew down from the mountains. Andi knew they were up high, but when they broke out of the forest and into a mountain meadow, she gasped. More peaks loomed in the distance. It seemed like they went on forever.

"I wonder what's on the other side," she mused aloud, her gaze fixed on the mountains.

"Nevada," Cory said. He bit off a chunk of jerky. There hadn't been time to stop and eat a decent meal.

"I know it's Nevada," Andi retorted. "I wonder what it's like."

"More mountains," Mitch said. "The desert, a few trees. Not much else."

"And Lake Tahoe," Cory added. "Don't forget Lake Tahoe."

"I'd like a lake right here," Jenny chimed in. "I bet there's good fishing in these mountain lakes."

Mitch grinned. "There certainly is. There's a lake over that way"— he waved his hand to the south—"with trout the length of your arm."

Cory raised a clenched fist. "I'm more interested in creeks that give up gold nuggets as big as this."

"Don't worry, Cory," Mitch said. "We'll more than likely be setting up camp tonight in one of those out-of-the-way shacks Mrs. Simmons told us about. I remember something like that the last time I was roaming these parts." He chuckled. "You'll get another chance to add to your treasure."

An hour later, the trail rose steeply and was joined by a rushing creek. It tumbled past the travelers in its race down the mountainside. One look at the noisy, churning water dashed Andi's hopes of leisurely panning for gold. "This creek's in an awful hurry to get where it's going," she joked to Cory.

"It's no use panning here," Cory muttered.

"Don't judge the whole creek by one part," Mitch warned with a smile. "The trail levels off eventually. I think you'll like what you find."

Cory and Andi brightened at that. Jenny slumped.

"You can fish with me, Jenny," Mitch offered. "Let Cory and Andi pan for gold, and we'll get supper. Or"—he gave the girl a quick, teasing wink—"what do you say we cook up that rattlesnake for supper? We don't want it to go bad, you know."

Jenny shuddered and gave Mitch a look that was far from respectful. Andi laughed.

As Mitch had promised, the trail leveled off about an hour later. The creek quieted to a gently gurgling stream. The water looked so tempting that Andi brought Taffy to a stop and waved at the others to stop too. The horses dipped their noses in the creek and drank deeply.

"Does this creek run by the cabin?" Andi asked.

"I think so." Mitch dismounted and ducked his head in the water. He came up shivering.

Andi laughed and slid off her horse. She cupped her hands and took a drink of the clearest water she had seen yet.

"It's so *cold!*"

"Come on," Mitch said, mounting his horse. "The cabin's not far. I think it's just around the other side of that small hill of boulders and scrub pine."

Andi was glad they were almost there. Her stomach was beginning to growl for fresh fish—or even for snake. She'd been more interested in enjoying the view and talking with her friends than digging around in her saddlebags for a lousy piece of beef jerky for lunch.

She was arguing with Cory about gold panning techniques when Mitch suddenly reined in his horse and put up a hand. Andi closed her mouth and put a finger to her lips to warn Jenny not to talk. She pulled Taffy to a halt and dismounted. Cory and Jenny quietly followed suit. They tied their horses to a scrub pine and waited.

Mitch had dismounted and was standing a couple dozen yards farther up the trail. When he looked back at them, Andi's mouth fell open. Her brother's face was set in an expression she knew well. Something was wrong.

In a flash, she was by his side. "What's the matter?"

Mitch frowned and motioned her back.

Andi obeyed at once. She scurried back to her friends and led them around a rocky outcropping the size of a small cabin.

"What's going on?" Cory demanded.

"I don't know," Andi said, "but something's not right."

A minute later Mitch joined them behind the rock. "The cabin's in the clearing, about a hundred yards past these rocks, but . . ."

"But what?" Andi asked.

"It's not empty. There're a couple of horses in the corral, and smoke's coming from the chimney."

A pang of disappointment stabbed Andi. No camping in a cabin next to a gold creek tonight. "So we don't get to stay here?"

"Not in the cabin. Maybe we can set up camp by the creek."

Cory and Jenny groaned.

Mitch glanced up at the sun. "It's getting late. If I'd known this place was occupied, I would have picked a different spot. There's nothing suitable for five or six miles back down the trail—too steep. Perhaps the folks in the cabin will let us camp here. Or maybe they know a good spot farther up. I'll find out."

Andi nodded. "Good idea. Let's go."

"Hold on, sis." Mitch put out a hand to keep her in place. "You and your friends are staying right here until I get back."

"But why? You might need our help."

"I don't need your help to knock on a cabin door," Mitch said with a grin. "Chances are it's a poor squatter family with ten kids, but you're still staying here."

Andi relaxed. "All right. But be quick. I'm getting hungry."

But Mitch didn't leave. He reached into his saddlebag and pulled out his gun belt. He secured it around his hips, pulled the Colt .45 from its holster, and examined it. Then he replaced the pistol in his holster and reached for his rifle, which so far had gone unused the entire trip.

Andi watched Mitch's preparations with wide eyes. "You don't need all that to talk to a family of squatters, do you?"

"Probably not. But I like to be prepared." He held out the rifle. "Besides, the rifle's for you. You're my backup."

Andi wrapped her hands around the cold, hard metal of the rifle. "Your backup?" Her throat went dry. "Your backup for what?"

Mitch let out a breath. "Some mighty peculiar folks live back in these hills. Most don't take kindly to strangers. If the people who've taken over that shack are the shoot-first-ask-questions-later type, I don't want them to get past me and come looking for you and your friends." He held Andi's gaze. "Don't be afraid to use it, sis."

Andi set the butt of the rifle on the ground. "I'm not afraid. It's . . . well . . . you know how I shoot."

Mitch chuckled. "That's true. Annie Oakley you're not." Chad had given up trying to teach Andi how to shoot straight. The lessons usually ended in arguments and tears.

Andi shook her head. "I don't make a very good backup man." She turned to Cory and handed him the rifle. "You be the backup man."

Cory looked at Mitch before taking the rifle from Andi. When Mitch nodded, Cory said, "I shoot pretty good. When I go on the jack rabbit hunt each year, I bag dozens and dozens of the pesky critters."

"I don't expect to find any jack rabbits around here," Mitch said, "but anyone who sees you holding a rifle at gut-level will probably back off."

Cory grinned and nodded.

Andi glanced from the rifle in Cory's arms to her brother. "You know, Mitch, a backup man's no good if he's out of sight. You should take Cory along."

Mitch reached out and took Andi by the shoulders. "I need you *all* to stay here, and I don't want any argument about it." His voice had turned hard.

"Why are you getting so worked up? You knock on the door, ask them if we can stay, and that's that."

"We're in the middle of nowhere, Andi. I don't know who's in that cabin. It might be a poor, friendly squatter family. Then again, it may not be. If I could turn around and take you all back I would. But it's getting too late. We have to stay here—somewhere—so we're doing this my way."

Andi glanced at her friends. Cory and Jenny stood off to the side. Cory looked raring to go, confident of his skills with the rifle. Jenny, on the other hand, looked sick.

Mitch turned Andi back to face him. "Do as I say, all right?"

"What about *you*?"

"Never mind about me. Promise me that you'll stay here, out of sight."

"Please, Mitch, don't make me promise," Andi pleaded. Promises had a way of coming back to haunt her, because real life never happened the way most folks planned. Promises sometimes got twisted, and she ended up in trouble with her conscience. She didn't want to be wrestling with herself over whether she should break a promise or not. Not today.

Mitch sighed. "Fine." He looked at Cory. "Mr. Blake, keep my sister from doing anything foolhardy while I'm away, would you? If things go wrong—like if you hear shots being fired—take care of the girls and get them back to town as soon as you can."

Cory clutched the rifle tighter in his hands and nodded. "I'll look after them, Mitch."

"Good." Mitch relaxed. He pulled the brim of Andi's hat over her eyes in fun. "I didn't mean to scare you, sis. Likely we'll have a good laugh over this at supper. But I've heard too many tales about the backcountry not to take a few precautions."

Andi pushed the hat out of her eyes and looked up at him. "Hurry back."

"You bet." He turned away from the group, rounded a bend in the trail, and disappeared.

Chapter Eight

TWO-LEGGED SNAKES

As soon as Mitch was out of sight, Andi scrambled to the top of a large boulder. From there she tried to peer through the trees. She could make out a hint of a clearing, but no shack popped into view. She sighed, cupped her chin in her hands, and said, "I hope Mitch hurries. I don't know about you two, but my belly's hollering for supper."

Cory and Jenny joined her on the outcropping. There was plenty of room. Cory dragged the rifle behind him and stood up, assuming the position of a guard in a watch tower. Andi tilted her head back and squinted up at him. "Who are you, an army scout at Fort Laramie?"

Jenny giggled.

Cory glared at her. "If you remember, Mitch put me in charge of you girls. I take my duties seriously."

"I can see that," Andi snickered. "You make a fine target up there for any desperado to take a shot at." When she saw the set look on his face, she relented. After all, she'd given the rifle to Cory herself. "I'm sorry for teasing you, Cory. I know you won't let Mitch down."

Cory settled himself beside the girls and whispered, "Noise travels a fair piece in the mountains. We'd better keep quiet 'til Mitch comes back."

Andi nodded. She reached out and slapped at a whining mosquito, then returned to watching the deserted trail. Except for the rippling sound of the nearby creek, all was silent. There was no breeze, and the smell of the pine forest rose hot and dry in her nostrils. With a sigh of impatience, she slid from the boulder and settled on the ground. She leaned her head against the huge rock. "I wish Mitch would—"

"You in the cabin. Howdy!" Mitch's voice cracked like a gunshot in the quiet forest.

Andi jumped up, heart pounding. She listened for a response.

With a scraping sound and a *thud*, Cory slid from the outcropping and joined her. He lifted the rifle.

"Yeah?" a rough male voice growled. "What d'ya want?"

Andi's mouth went dry at the sound. It was a mean voice, full of suspicion. It certainly didn't sound like a poor squatter exchanging a friendly howdy. She closed her eyes and sent up a prayer for Mitch's safety. Then she took a step up the trail.

Cory's fingers curled around her arm. "Where are you going?"

"I want to get closer. How will we know if something's gone wrong if we can't see what's happening?" It sounded reasonable. After all, she hadn't promised anything.

Jenny slid down from the boulder and stared at Andi as if she were out of her mind. "You're crazy, Andi. We should stay put."

Andi turned on her friend. "What if he were *your* brother, Jenny? Would you stand around and do nothing?" She twisted free of Cory's grip and latched on to the rifle. "Give me the rifle and you can stay here."

Cory shook his head. He yanked the firearm out of Andi's grasp. "Mitch'll have my hide if I let you go off alone and do such a fool thing. I . . . I'm coming too." Hoisting the rifle in front of him, he followed Andi along the path. "Stay with the horses, Jenny."

The cabin came into view. It stood in a small clearing, surrounded by pine trees and jagged rock formations. A rough enclosure, fashioned from fallen limbs, passed as a poor corral, where two horses watched Mitch. On the other side of the clearing, the creek bubbled nosily. It was a pretty spot—the perfect camp site for weary travelers. As she slipped into hiding behind a cluster of small pines, old logs, and boulders, Andi couldn't help but feel a stab of disappointment that the shack was occupied.

She peeked through the trees and brush. Mitch stood a good distance back from the shack. She hoped he couldn't see her.

"If Mitch finds out about this, our lives won't be worth a plugged nickel," Cory hissed in Andi's ear. "We see what's going on and then we get out of here."

Andi ignored him.

The door to the shack opened a crack, and the shadow of a man appeared. "What's yer business?" he roared through the opening.

"Just saying howdy," Mitch answered. He pushed his hat back and spread his hands in a friendly gesture. "I'm passing through and would like to spend the night next to your creek, if you don't mind."

The door flew open, and the owner of the rough voice showed himself. "I *do* mind." He lifted his rifle and aimed it at Mitch's chest. "Now clear out."

Andi clapped a hand over her mouth to keep from screaming. This was no ordinary, down-on-his luck squatter. This was a huge, ugly mountain of a man. Even from her hiding place, she could see his filthy, disheveled clothing and the long, greasy hanks of hair. He held the rifle in both hands, and a gun-belt hung loosely around his hips. His presence made every nerve in Andi's body tingle with fear. She'd rather sleep beside a boulder than be beholden to a mean-faced giant like this man.

"No need to point your rifle at me." Mitch raised his hands and backed up. "I'm leaving. I don't want any trouble. I'd heard this place was abandoned and—"

"You heard wrong." A wicked grin split the man's face. He spat a stream of tobacco juice in Mitch's direction.

Mitch took a few more steps backward. The man didn't lower his rifle, nor did the smile leave his face. He simply waited.

"Hurry, Mitch," Andi whispered. Something was wrong. The huge man seemed to be waiting for something, unwilling to let Mitch turn and walk away. Why? It tickled the back of her mind until she realized there were two horses in the corral. Where was the owner of the other horse?

Cory jabbed her in the shoulder. "Look up there." He pointed to a ragged, broken cliff behind Mitch. A man was creeping along the ridge. He stopped and raised a pistol at her brother's back.

There was no time to decide if yelling was a good idea or not. If she didn't warn Mitch, he'd be ambushed. She opened her mouth to shout, but Cory was faster. He clapped a hand over her mouth. "Don't you *dare* holler." Then he let her go, brought up the rifle, and pulled the trigger. The bullet struck the ledge of the outcropping with a loud *crack*. Splintered rock flew everywhere. The man balancing on the edge of the cliff stumbled and plunged to the ground below with bone-crushing finality.

Cory ducked behind a scattering of boulders and deadwood, dragging Andi with him. A loud curse and a volley of gunfire shattered the silence. Andi cringed. Together she and Cory lay flattened on the ground, not daring to move. Her face felt crushed against the carpet of pine needles and twigs. Her heart raced out of control. Had Cory's distraction warned Mitch in time?

Another shot. "Rob, you all right?" There was no answer.

Andi raised her head and peered between the branches and brush. The man from the cabin crouched behind the corral, but where was Mitch? She lifted her head higher, but she still couldn't see him. The next moment, the gunman darted from his hiding place. Andi dropped her head to the ground. She squeezed her eyes shut. *Please don't let him see us,* she pleaded silently.

The crunching of footsteps on loose rocks was followed by gunfire. Andi hoped it was Mitch's gunfire. She trembled. Cory's hand on her shoulder didn't stop her from shaking, but it kept her from screaming. She chanced a quick peek. The man now squatted behind the rocks at the base of the cliff, peering down at something. When he looked up, Andi caught her breath. Cold fury covered his face. He glanced in their direction and fired two shots.

"You and your pal in the woods are gonna pay for killin' Rob," he growled.

Mitch's voice came from the opposite side of the clearing. "It was an accident. He lost his balance and fell. We both saw what happened. Go back to the shack. I'll clear out. There's no need for more bloodshed."

At the sound of Mitch's voice, the man whirled and ducked behind an outcropping. Gunfire rang out. Andi flinched and flattened herself against the ground once again. Cory tugged at her sleeve. "Let's get out of here," he mouthed.

Andi knew this was the "something wrong" Mitch had warned them about back at the boulder before he left. She, Cory, and Jenny should have high-tailed it down the trail at the sound of the first gunshot. *But if we had,* Andi thought, *Mitch would be dead.* She shook her head at Cory. She couldn't move. She was too scared to think.

The gunfire continued, accompanied every few seconds by enraged swearing and shouting from the gunman. Would it never stop?

One more shot sounded. A final curse. Then silence.

Chapter Nine

AN IMPOSSIBLE TASK

Andi slowly lifted her head from the ground and peered toward the cabin. All was still. There was no sound except for the scolding of a chipmunk and the noisy creek. She could not see Mitch or the gunman. The clearing was empty. Where had they gone? Were they lurking in the surrounding forest, playing a deadly waiting game?

Several minutes passed. Andi pulled herself to a sitting position and brushed the dead grass and pine needles from her hair. She wanted to rush out and look for Mitch, but fear rooted her to the spot.

Cory sat up and lifted the rifle to his lap. His eyes were wide and troubled. "I don't like the looks of this," he whispered.

Andi didn't answer. She didn't like the looks or feel of anything. It was quiet. *Too* quiet. She sat in the eerie silence and waited for a sound—any sound—that told her someone was still alive. *Where are you, Mitch?*

Crack! A branch snapped. Andi whirled, heart pounding. A doe and her fawn stood no more than a stone's throw away. At the sight of Andi and Cory, they bounded into the brush. Andi's racing heart slowed. She sagged in relief. She'd half-expected to see the huge man pointing a gun at her.

"We're leaving," Cory said. Without waiting for Andi to agree, he snatched up the rifle and slipped away from their hiding place. Andi followed. She was too frightened to stay behind by herself. They scurried to the safety of the huge boulder, which only a short time before had seemed like the dullest place on earth. Now it looked like a welcome, safe haven.

Jenny met them as they rounded the bend in the trail. "I heard shots and . . . and . . ." She threw her arms around Andi. "Oh, Andi, I thought you were killed! I didn't bargain for this."

"None of us did," Cory said. He put down the rifle in disgust. "If that mean-lookin' fella from the cabin doesn't find and kill us, Mitch certainly will." He leaned against the boulder and crossed his arms. "I failed miserably in taking care of you girls. I should have kept you here, Andi, even if I had to sit on you."

"You saved Mitch's life, Cory. That other gunman was going to shoot him. I think he'll forgive you for following him." Andi pulled away from Jenny. "But what do we do now? Everything's so quiet, so scary. What are they up to? Why isn't anyone shooting?"

"I'd be glad about that if I were you," Jenny said. "This trip is getting more dangerous by the day. First a rattlesnake. Now a couple of crazy fellows taking pot shots at your brother. What next?"

Chase whinnied loudly, and Andi froze. It was a sound that could easily be heard from the clearing around the cabin. Surely someone would come and check it out. But no one appeared.

"Why doesn't Mitch come back?" Andi asked.

Cory shrugged. "Maybe he's sneaking around, hiding, trying to slip past that fellow. Or maybe he got away and he's circling around to meet up with us back here."

Andi bit her lip in thought. Then she took a deep breath. "I'm scared, but I have to see what happened to Mitch."

Cory stepped in the trail and blocked Andi's way. "You ran off once on a fool's errand, but you're not gonna do it twice. Mitch told me to get you girls to Fresno Flats in one piece and that's what I aim to do. He can catch up later." He held her gaze, daring her to argue with him.

Andi realized with a shock that Cory towered over her by a full head. Why hadn't she noticed that before? Only a year ago, she and Cory were close in size. Now it appeared that he'd shot up all at once. She looked at the set expression on his face and knew she wouldn't get past Cory a second time. She needed his cooperation.

"But what if Mitch didn't get away? What if he's hurt? We can't run away and leave him lying in the middle of nowhere." She pointed at the sky. "Besides, it's nearly dusk. We'd never make it down that trail in the dark, and you know it. We're stuck here for the night, so we might as well go and see what happened." She paused. "Please."

Cory let out a long, uncertain sigh and nodded. "You're right about not being able to go anywhere tonight. We'll have to huddle behind the outcropping and make the best of it, then head for town at first light."

"What about Mitch?" Andi insisted.

"All right," Cory said. "I'll go. I've got the rifle. I'll sneak up as close as I can and see what happened, but you and Jenny have to stay here."

"Suits me," Jenny said. She dropped to the ground and leaned against the rock. "My head's pounding, and my shoulder hurts something fierce. A bite to eat and Mrs. Simmons's chatter is looking pretty good to me right about now."

At the words "bite to eat," Andi's stomach rumbled. She was hungry too. She was torn between trying to convince Cory to let her go along and staying behind to care for her friend. Finally, she gave in. "All right, Cory. You go. But you'd better come back in a hurry."

"Yes, *ma'am.*" He gave her a snappy salute. Then he whirled and headed up the trail.

Andi opened her saddlebags and pulled out a few pieces of jerky and two apples. She snagged her canteen from around the saddle horn and plopped down beside Jenny, dumping the food in her lap. "It's not much, but chances are there will be no trout tonight. We'll have to make do with what we've got." Giving the jerky a look of distaste, she bit off a chunk and started chewing.

Jenny accepted the food with a nod. She sat quietly, eating the jerky. Andi looked at Jenny in concern. Her spunky friend usually had plenty to say, and she wasn't afraid to speak her mind. She was probably hurting more than she wanted to admit. If things hadn't gone so horribly wrong, right now they would have been resting along the creek bank, fishing or panning for a little gold before sundown. Jenny would have had a decent bed to sleep in tonight instead of huddling on the back side of a cold, rough rock. And Mitch would . . .

Hot tears sprang to Andi's eyes at the thought of her brother. Where was he? Where was—?

"Andi! Get over here. Quick!"

Cory's shout propelled Andi to her feet in an instant. She tore along the trail at a dead run, leaving Jenny behind to fend for herself. *Please, God, let Mitch be all right.* She didn't have time to add anything more to her frantic prayer. She broke into the clearing and saw no one.

"Over here," Cory bellowed from behind the corral.

Andi sailed around the corral and stopped short. Cory was crouched over a figure behind some deadwood. He looked up at Andi's approach, his face ashen. "It's Mitch. He . . . he . . . I think he's been shot."

With a cry of disbelief, Andi sank to the ground beside her brother. He lay on his stomach, still as death. His face was streaked with blood from a scrape. Her heart hammered. *He can't be dead. He can't be!* A sob caught in her throat.

Cory laid a hand on her arm. "He's alive, Andi. I checked. But he's hurt bad. Take a look." He pointed at Mitch's legs. One trouser leg was soaked with dark red blood.

Andi tried to think. What should she do? Mitch was bleeding, perhaps bleeding to death. Was there a bullet in his leg? How would she ever get the bleeding stopped? Suddenly, a new thought made her heart race faster.

"W-where's the other man?" She tried desperately to keep her stomach under control. She was glad she hadn't eaten much jerky. If she had, it would have been right there on the ground in front of her.

"Dead," Cory said in a flat voice. "We're safe for now. But we've got to get Mitch into the shack so we can see how bad off he is." When she didn't answer, he shook her arm. "You hear me, Andi?"

Andi was staring at her brother's white, blood-streaked face. She jumped at Cory's touch. "I know." But she didn't move.

A gasp from behind brought Andi around.

Jenny stood above them, staring. She held a piece of jerky in one hand. The canteen was slung over her good shoulder. "What happened?"

Andi ignored her question. She looked at Mitch and blinked back tears. She couldn't cry. Not now. Not yet. What had Cory said? What did they need to do?

Cory stood and yanked Andi up beside him. "Listen. This is what we're going to do. Andi, you and Jenny each take an arm and pull. I'll see if I can lift his legs. It's no more than a stone's throw to the shack. Between the three of us, we should be able to get him inside."

As Andi staggered under her share of Mitch's dead weight, she wondered what she would have done without Cory and Jenny's help. Her friends were panting, struggling to carry the limp body. Twice they faltered, sending Mitch to the hard ground with a *thud*. He moaned.

"Hang on, Mitch," Andi said. "Hang on for a couple more minutes. We're almost there." She glanced past Cory and saw the trail of blood they were sprinkling behind. She gulped. So much blood.

"Over here," she heard Cory pant as they crossed the threshold of the shack. The late afternoon sun streamed through the doorway. They half-carried, half-dragged Mitch to a bunk bed against the far wall. The bottom bunk was little more than a large, rough cot in need of repair. Its straw mattress was lumpy and torn, but it was better than the ground, and the bedding looked relatively clean.

Mitch let out a low, pain-filled moan as Andi settled him on the bunk. His breath came in shallow gasps. His lip was bloody, and his face scratched and filthy. Andi reached into her back pocket and pulled out her bandana. Without a word, Jenny held out the canteen. Andi soaked the wide cloth and began to gently wipe away the blood from his face. "Wake up, Mitch. We got you inside. Wake up." When there was no response, she dribbled water from the canteen onto his head.

Mitch opened his eyes and gasped.

Andi saw fear and anguish in his blue gaze. "What are we going to do, Mitch?" She glanced at his blood-soaked trouser leg. To her horror, blood was already seeping into the bedding under him.

Mitch licked his lips. "I think . . . the bullet went . . . clean through my leg." His voice shook. "That's the good news." He gave Andi a lopsided smile.

Andi wasn't fooled. Not one bit. Bullet or no bullet, the blood was still trickling out. "What's good about *that*?"

"You don't . . . have to take . . . a bullet out of my leg," Mitch said between breaths. "But I'm losing a lot of blood. You've got to stop . . . the bleeding." He closed his eyes and shuddered, clearly trying to control the pain long enough to talk.

Andi gaped at Mitch. She didn't know the first thing about how to stop the flow. She tore her gaze away from her brother long enough to look at her friends. They stood at the end of the bunk, watching and waiting. *Waiting for what?* Andi wondered. *Waiting for me to tell them what to do? I don't know what to do.*

She turned back to Mitch. Her voice caught. "N-no, Mitch. I can't do it. There's too much blood. You need a doctor or . . . or Mrs. Simmons. Yes, we'll fetch Mrs. Simmons. She'll know what to do. I don't know anything about fixing bullet holes." She started to cry. "I'll . . . I'll kill you for sure and—"

Mitch clamped a viselike grip around Andi's wrist. "Stop crying. Do you hear me? Stop it!" He gave her a shake.

Andi gulped back her tears and stared at her brother. Mitch had never spoken to her like this before.

"Listen to me, little sister." His face was contorted in pain, but his voice suddenly turned strong and clear. "I've only got one chance to make it off this mountain, and you're going to give me that chance. If you don't stop the bleeding, I'll *die*. Now quit your bawling and do it. I'm counting on you. Do you understand me?" His grip tightened.

Andi winced at the pain. She nodded, too scared of this new Mitch to do anything else.

"Good. No matter how loud I yell, you plug your ears and get the job done. If I'm real lucky, I'll pass out." Then his voice softened. "I know you're scared, sis, but right now you're better than any doctor because"—he smiled weakly—"because you're all I've got. Now get to it."

His hand fell limply to his side.

Chapter Ten

THE DARKEST HOUR

Andi rubbed her sore wrist, took a deep breath, and looked at her friends. Her eyes welled up with tears, but she brushed a sleeve across her face and took charge. "We have to cut his trouser leg off."

Her fingers shook as she fished around in her overalls for her pocketknife. Trembling, she pulled it out and opened the blade. She reached for the blood-soaked trousers. Slick, sticky liquid oozed between her fingers when she lifted the fabric away from Mitch's leg. Choking back the bile that rose in her throat, she drove the knife into the heavy denim. It made a dull ripping sound.

"Here, let me help," Cory offered. He stood beside her and plunged his own knife into the other side of the jeans. Sawing and slipping, they worked their way around the fabric until the leg was exposed. Cory sliced the trouser leg clear to the boot and yanked it away. It fell to the floor with a *splat*.

Andi nearly gagged. A large, dark red-and-black hole oozed blood from the fleshy part of her brother's swollen thigh. Andi exchanged a horrified look with Cory.

"You can do it," Cory whispered his encouragement. "I know you can."

Mitch was right. The bullet had either missed or grazed the bone and gone out the back of his leg. How could she stop the blood from both sides at once? She glanced at Mitch. His eyes were closed, and his face was as pale as death. She shook him. "Mitch? Wake up. We got the trouser cut off."

Mitch came to. "How does it . . . look?" He tried to sit up, but fell back with a groan.

"Terrible," Andi whispered.

"Whiskey," Mitch managed to say. "Douse the leg. Best we can do . . . for now. Then find something clean to . . . to plug the holes." His eyes closed.

Cory leaped away to look for the whiskey. Andi heard him fumbling around across the room, but she couldn't watch. Her gaze was riveted on her brother as she fished around in her back pocket for her bandana. Then she remembered. She'd used it to clean off Mitch's face. It lay, stained with blood and dirt, on the floor beside her feet.

Cory returned triumphant, with a half-empty bottle of amber liquid in his hand. His grin vanished when Andi said through clenched teeth, "Pour it on."

The only sound Mitch made when Cory dumped the contents of the whiskey bottle over his leg was a sharp intake of breath. But Andi noticed his fists were tightly clenched and his face was a mask of agony.

Without being told, Cory pulled a large bandana from his pocket and wadded it up. He pressed it firmly against one of the wounds. "Quick. Use yours to plug the other hole."

"I can't. It's filthy," Andi said.

Jenny stuffed a cloth in her hand. "Here, use mine." She had lit a kerosene lamp and stood near the bed, holding it high. Until then, Andi hadn't realized how dark and gloomy it was inside the cabin.

"My belt," Mitch said in a shaky voice. "Use it to keep the bandages in place. You'll have to . . . to cinch it up tight at first until the bleeding slows. But remember . . ." His voice trailed off. He closed his eyes.

Andi shook him. "Remember what?"

"Remember to keep an eye on things. If the belt stays too tight for too long, I'll . . . lose my leg." He opened his eyes. "I'd prefer that didn't happen." Again, the lopsided grin.

Andi's heart skipped a beat. Where did Mitch find the strength to ignore what must be agonizing pain and instead try to lighten the mood?

"The longer you wait, the more blood he's gonna lose," Cory said, breaking into her thoughts. "We can't sit here all night holding these bandanas in place. I'll help you all I can, but he's *your* brother. You gotta do it."

Andi turned back to Mitch. "How will I know if the belt's too tight?"

There was no answer.

"Mitch!" Afraid that Mitch might bleed to death right before her eyes, she let go of the bandana she was pressing against the wound and fumbled desperately at her brother's waist. She unbuckled the gun belt and tried to toss it aside. It was too bulky to remove. Jenny set aside the lamp and lent a shaky hand. Together the girls managed to yank the bulky holster away and let it fall to the ground.

Andi loosened the belt and pulled. Unlike the holster, it slipped easily through the belt loops and was soon dangling from her hand. Clenching her jaw, she wiggled and prodded the belt until she had worked it under Mitch's thigh. Then she grasped both ends and made a loop. Mitch didn't move. Determined to ignore Mitch if he hollered, Andi nodded to Cory. He held both wads of cloth firmly in place as Andi threaded the belt through the buckle. Then she paused and closed her eyes. *Please make this work, God.* She opened her eyes and began to cinch up the belt. Cory moved his fingers out of the way as it tightened against the makeshift bandages.

"Tighter," Cory said when she paused. "It's gotta keep everything in place. Mitch might move, and it could slip off. You can't let that happen."

Andi tightened the belt another notch, and Mitch's whole body shuddered. But he didn't holler. He was out cold, for which Andi was thankful. She didn't think she could have continued if he'd yelled or thrashed around.

"That's good," Cory said. "Buckle it."

Andi's fingers fumbled as she guided the metal piece into the hole. "I-I think I'm going to be sick."

"Not yet," Cory said. "Look. It's working."

Andi swallowed hard and looked at Mitch's leg. The bandages were red with blood, but no more seemed to be oozing out. "It *is* working," she whispered in awe.

"And Mitch is still unconscious, which is good," Cory added.

Thank you. Andi breathed her quiet prayer, then turned away from the bunk and looked down at her hands. They were sticky with blood. Her stomach turned over. With a desperate gulp, Andi dashed across the shack and out the door. She barely made it around the corner before she lost what little food she'd eaten earlier that afternoon. When her stomach was empty, she leaned over the corral railing and sobbed. The bleeding had stopped—for now—but the ordeal was far from over. She would eventually have to loosen the belt or Mitch might lose his leg. Would the wounds start bleeding again?

Worn out in body and spirit, she sank to the ground and sat in the twilight, weeping.

A few minutes later, she heard the quiet footsteps of someone approaching. Without a word, Jenny knelt beside Andi and pulled her into a tight embrace. "Cry all you want, Andi. But it's not always good to cry alone. That's what friends are for." There were tears in her eyes.

Andi sobbed. It did feel good to cry on Jenny's shoulder. What if she and Mitch had been up here alone? No, she wouldn't think about that. Instead, she thanked God for good friends like Jenny and Cory. Together they'd get through this. God had given her the strength to endure the worst part.

When her tears finally ended, Andi untangled herself from Jenny's embrace and leaned back against the corral railing. "Thank you," she said simply.

Jenny scooted beside her and rested against a post. "You're welcome." She shook her head. "That was really something, Andi. You sure made a better job of it than I ever could. I have to confess that I can't abide being around blood and the like. Truth be told, I've never seen what I've seen today."

Andi looked at Jenny in surprise. "Neither have I. Things like this don't happen on the ranch. Oh, there are plenty of accidents, but there's always someone around who knows what to do." She took a deep breath. "Until today, I'd never seen a gunshot wound up close like that, right after it happened. Last year I didn't know I'd been shot until it was all over."

Jenny sighed. "It's the same with me. When Eli got stitched up, I didn't watch. I ran and hid in my room until Mama took care of it. I heard him hollering, and that was enough for me. I reckon I'm not cut out to be a logger's wife. I couldn't do what my mother did." She gave Andi's hand a squeeze. "I couldn't do what you did, either."

"Yes, you could," Andi replied quietly. She brushed an arm across her wet face. "You could if you loved your brother as much as I love mine, and if he scared you enough to realize you were his only chance." She looked up. A handful of stars dusted the dark blue expanse above her. It was getting late. The sun had dipped below the mountains, and an evening chill nipped the air. It was time to return to the shack and check on Mitch. She took hold of the railing and pulled herself up. "Let's go inside."

Andi stepped through the doorway and found Cory sitting beside Mitch. He'd lit another lamp and set it on an overturned crate next to the bunk. It gave off a pale-yellow glow that did little to light the dingy place. Cory had also found a rough covering and spread it over Mitch. He saw the girls and jumped up from his stool. "You can sit here," he offered, waving Andi over. "I've been watching. He hasn't twitched an eyelash since we put the belt on, but he's still breathing. You can see his chest move up and down."

"Thanks." Andi slumped on the stool, drained. She poured water from the canteen over her hands and wiped them off on her overalls the best she could.

Cory headed for the door.

"Where are you going?" Andi asked. "It's getting late."

"Somebody's got to take care of the horses and bring in the supplies."

Andi leaped up in horror. "Taffy! How could I have forgotten my horse? It's been *hours*." Taffy and the other horses were down the trail, probably still tied up to the scrub pine. She groaned.

"Take it easy," Cory said. "You've had plenty on your mind. It might feel like it's been hours, but it's not as late as you think. You stay with Mitch, and Jenny and I will look after the horses. I want to do it while there's still some light. We'll settle them in the corral with the other horses. It won't take long."

"Jenny's not well," Andi said. "Her shoulder and head aren't healed yet. She needs to rest."

Jenny waved away Andi's concern. "I want to help." Before Andi could protest, she followed Cory out the door.

Alone with her brother, Andi had a chance to look around at what would most certainly be their home for the next several days. Even if Mitch managed to survive the crude nursing care, he wouldn't be riding a horse for some time. Andi cringed. She didn't want to think that far ahead. It took too much energy. She shoved tomorrow's problems into a back corner of her mind and glanced around the shack.

The two kerosene lamps gave off just enough light to see by. Andi could make out a table, a bench seat, and a couple of backless stools in the middle of the cabin. Across the room, the shack's only window opened out to the darkening night. Below the window, a shelf held a few bottles of whiskey, tins of what Andi hoped contained decent food, and a small sack of flour. An assortment of cups, tin plates, and forks lay piled up in a large pan on the counter. They were surrounded by opened cans of beans and other, unrecognizable contents. Dozens of flies buzzed around the exposed food, feasting on the mess. There was no sink and no pump. Water would have to be hauled up from the creek.

Across from the doorway, the fireplace took up a good portion of the wall. Its gaping hole showed a bed of ashes. A round, black pot hung over the dead fire from a metal rod. Hunger pangs forced Andi to leave her place beside Mitch to see if there was anything in the pot fit to eat. When she lifted the lid, a sour odor drifted up. Gagging, she slammed the lid down and returned to the stool. She wasn't hungry anymore. With a sigh, she decided this filthy shack in the middle of nowhere was without a doubt the most dismal place she had ever seen.

To keep her mind off all the work she and her friends would have to do to make the shack a decent place to stay, Andi turned to Mitch and gingerly lifted the blanket. His leg was swollen, but as far as she could tell, there was no new blood. What now? How long should she wait before she loosened the belt and hoped the blood had clotted? An hour? Two hours? All night?

I wish Mother were here. She'd know what to do.

Andi shook her head. Wishing for her mother would make her start crying again. Mother wasn't here, and it wasn't likely she'd be seeing her any time soon. Then a horrible thought struck. What if Mitch didn't make it? Mother would never see him again.

The idea set her head spinning. "No!" She clenched her fist and slammed it into her palm. "That's not going to happen." With God's help, she would keep her brother alive. She wasn't sure how she was going to accomplish this, but the time for tears and self-pity was past. Mitch was right. She was his only chance, and she had a job to do. She gently tucked the blanket around Mitch's shoulders and planted a tender kiss on his cheek.

"Don't you worry, big brother. You're not going to die. Not if I can help it."

Chapter Eleven

A Shocking Discovery

A ndi woke with a start. *How long have I been asleep?* The kerosene lamp still burned, but from the chill in the cabin, Andi knew it must be late, maybe even close to dawn. She remembered only snatches from the evening before. She'd managed to stay awake long enough to wipe the rest of the dirt and blood from her brother's face and assure herself he was still breathing before she'd collapsed across the foot of the bed and into a dead sleep.

If it's close to dawn, then I've slept all night! Andi thought in panic. She crawled from her spot at Mitch's feet and reached for the covering. She'd intended to stay up and tend her brother through the night. She'd meant to loosen the belt. Now it looked like she'd failed. Andi's shaking hand gripped the blanket, afraid to lift it and discover what damage she'd done by falling asleep.

"I took care of it a few minutes ago." Cory's quiet words sent a wave of relief over Andi. He rose from his bedroll in front of the fireplace and joined her at Mitch's side. "It doesn't look too bad. I think it's clotting. A few more hours and the belt can probably stay on the last notch—to keep the bandages in place." He lifted the covering and motioned to the still-swollen leg. "I loosened it a bit and no blood came pouring out."

"You did that?" Andi marveled. "You stayed up all night tending his leg?"

"No, not all night. It's still pretty early. Besides, you did most of it. I took over when you woke me and told me you couldn't stay awake a minute longer." He gave her a puzzled look. "Don't you remember?"

Andi's mouth dropped open. Her mind was fuzzy. "No, I don't remember."

"Well, that doesn't surprise me none. You've surely had yourself a day." Cory grinned, but quickly became sober. "You were asleep when Jenny and I hauled in the supplies"—he indicated the bundles heaped next to the door—"but you woke up later and sat with Mitch for quite some time." He laughed at her look of dismay. "I took over an hour or two ago."

"Where's Jenny?" Andi asked.

Cory pointed to the bunk above Mitch. "Out cold. Her head was beginning to ache so she went to bed." He wandered over to his bedroll and plopped down. "I think Mitch'll be fine if we both go back to sleep. There's still a couple of hours until dawn. I need the rest 'cause at first light I'm leaving."

Andi's mind felt like a wet sponge, soggy with sleep. "What?"

"Go back to bed," Cory mumbled. "We'll talk about it in the morning."

When Andi opened her eyes the next time, a pale light was shining through the window on the far side of the room. She shivered. Summers in the mountains might be hot, but the nights were definitely chilly. She roused herself long enough to creep cautiously from the bed and fumble her way to the fireplace.

To her surprise, a small fire was crackling merrily. A stack of deadwood lay strewn in disarray a few feet from the fireplace. The door opened and Cory appeared, with his arms full of wood. He dumped it on the floor as quietly as he could and straightened up.

"This should hold you for today. There's plenty more wood outside, lying around for the taking. I've watered the horses and tossed them some hay. Believe it or not, there's a pile of hay around back, along with a privy and a lean-to." He grinned. "All the comforts of home."

Andi listened to Cory without saying a word. He must have been up for a while if he'd done all those chores. A fire. Extra wood. The horses tended. What else?

"I already ate," he continued when Andi didn't respond. "Flash is saddled and I'm ready to go."

Andi found her tongue at last. "Go? Where are you going?"

Cory took hold of Andi's shoulders and gave her a little shake. "Wake up, Andi. What's gotten into you? I'm going to town. Where did you think I was going? We can't stay here. Mitch needs better care than we can give him. He made it through the first night, but he's not out of the woods yet. I'm going for help."

Andi shook herself wide awake and nodded. "You're right."

"I'll bring back Mrs. Simmons to tend Mitch, as well as a couple of strong men who can pack him out on a stretcher or a travois." His expression turned grim. "They can also give those two dead fellas a proper burial. Doesn't seem decent to leave 'em lying out there." Then he smiled. "But never you mind about them. They're out of sight—I took care of that too—so you and Jenny don't have to worry about anything while I'm gone." Cory reached for a grub sack and flung it over his shoulder.

"You're fetching Mrs. Simmons? Don't you think she's kind of heavy to haul herself onto the back of a horse and ride all the way up here?"

Cory shook his head. "Naw. Mrs. Simmons strikes me as being spry as a young filly, even for all her extra padding. I can easily see her on a horse—a large one, mind you—tramping out to nurse a body no matter where he is. You'll see. She'll come."

"She'll talk your ear off all the way," Andi said with a laugh. It was the first time she'd laughed in over a day, and it felt good. It was a relief to hear Cory share his plans with such confidence. He had taken to heart Mitch's request to care for her and Jenny, and he looked like he was enjoying his new role. With Mitch laid up, the transformation from joking school chum to protector appeared complete.

With a sudden pang, Andi realized she didn't want Cory to leave. As soon as he disappeared down the trail, the responsibility would fall squarely on her young shoulders. She was still too weary to pick up that burden, but what choice did she have?

"I reckon I'll be on my way," Cory said. He ignored Andi's remark about Mrs. Simmons's tendency to prattle. "I should arrive in Fresno Flats this evening. First thing tomorrow morning, I'll head back with help. You can expect us sometime tomorrow evening—or the next morning at the very latest."

Andi looked at the floor. "I reckon."

Cory reached out and gave her braid a teasing yank. "Hey, don't worry. It's not like you're all alone. Jenny's here. You two will be so busy tending Mitch and fishing and panning for gold that the time will fly. Nobody's likely to come calling. Even if they do, you've got the rifle and Mitch's pistol."

Andi looked up. "Take Mitch's gun along."

Cory grinned. "What for? I don't intend to stop riding 'til I reach town. It's not likely I'll need to shoot anything on the trail."

"Cory, I'm scared," Andi admitted. "What if something happens to you? Then what?"

Cory gave her braid another tug. "If it makes you feel better, sure, I'll take it along." He scooped up the pistol, turned, and walked out the door. Andi followed.

Cory mounted Flash and gave Andi a cheerful wave. Then he headed down the trail to Fresno Flats . . . and help.

When Andi shuffled back inside the shack, she saw Jenny peering at her from the top of the bunk bed. Her unruly red tangles cascaded over the bed frame, and her bandage had slipped down over one eye, giving her a wild, rakish look. She shoved the ragged cloth up on her forehead and said, "So he's off to bring back help? He'd better hurry. This place makes me ill. It's filthy and not fit for decent folks."

Andi turned a full circle, giving the cabin a critical eye. Nothing had changed from her view of it the night before, except for the red embers left over from Cory's cheery blaze. Grasping the poker, she stirred up the dying fire and tossed in some wood from the generous pile. Instantly, the fire burst into a friendly flame. She fed it slowly until the blaze grew in light and heat.

"We're going to need this fire today, even though the sun will likely scorch us soon enough," she told Jenny. "We've got to eat, and the only pot for cooking is"—she swallowed at the memory of the rancid odor—"right here." She lifted the black beast from the metal rod and held it high. "Your choice, Jenny. Do you want to take care of Mitch and look for something fit to eat or do you want to take this disgusting pot outside and scour it in the creek?"

Jenny climbed down from the bunk. She was careful not to wobble it and disturb the pale, sleeping man below. "I'm going to scour more than that pot, now that Cory's left and your brother's asleep." She grinned. "I haven't had a decent wash since we left the ranch nearly a week ago."

"That's a swell idea," Andi agreed. She glanced down at her own clothes. Dried blood and dirt had combined to paint her overalls a dark, rusty red. "Do you think we might find a piece of soap somewhere around here?"

Jenny made a face. "How much do you want to bet that the pigs who wallowed in this dirty shack have never even seen soap?" Then she brightened. "But it's worth a try. You look after your brother and I'll see what I can find."

While Jenny began a thorough search for some soap, Andi hurried to Mitch's side. She lifted the blanket and was heartened to see that below his knee, the leg was a healthy flesh color—a good sign. It meant blood was flowing. In contrast, the wounded thigh above his knee was a mess. Plastered with old, dark blood, it looked worse in daylight than it had last night by kerosene lamp. The belt was securely cinched around the leg, holding the two bandages in place. But the wads were stiff with dried blood.

Andi didn't dare touch anything. Since the leg looked healthy, she needn't try and loosen the belt that held the makeshift bandages. Perhaps she should be dousing the wounds with whiskey? She shook her head and decided not to take any silly chances by pulling the bandages off. More than likely the clots would break open and Mitch would start bleeding all over again. "As dreadful as it looks, I'm leaving it alone," she decided with a shudder.

She laid a hand on his shoulder and gave him a gentle shake. "Mitch, can you hear me?" There was no response. She covered him up and turned to Jenny, anxious to find out if she had found any soap.

Jenny held up a small piece of brown lye soap. "It's the size of my big toe, but I think we can squeeze two quick washings out of it. I found it behind the pan of dishes, buried out of sight under mounds of dirty rags." She snatched up her clean clothes and the cooking pot and scampered out the door.

Andi was waiting when Jenny returned. She accepted what was left of the soap, dug through her saddlebags, and pulled out a change of clothes. She threw the clothing over her shoulder and headed for the creek, where she stripped off her filthy overalls and stepped into the chilly water. As she scrubbed away the dirt and blood, she let the icy water do its work of refreshing both her body and spirit. "He's going to be all right," she told herself while she dressed—still wet—in fresh clothes. She'd managed to complete a nearly impossible task last night, and the bleeding bullet hole was a quickly fading memory. Her spirits rose. "Cory'll come back with help and Mitch will be fine."

Andi pulled her boots on, left her old clothes to soak in the creek,

and started back to the cabin, feeling almost cheerful. She was hum-
ming "Home on the Range" and thinking that everything would
be perfect if only Mitch would wake up, when she spotted Jenny
running toward her.

"Andi!" Jenny grabbed her arm, panting. "You gotta come quick.
Oh, what are we going to do?"

Andi's stomach lurched. "Is Mitch all right?"

Jenny yanked on Andi's arm. "As far as I know. He hasn't made
a peep." She took a deep breath. "It's something I found. I was poking around, looking for food under the bed, and I found . . ." She
paused, for the girls had reached the shack. They hurried inside. "I
found . . . this."

Andi stared, speechless. Jenny had piled half a dozen sacks in the
middle of the rough table. Printed in bold, black letters were the words:

FRESNO COUNTY BANK.

Chapter Twelve

UNWANTED TREASURE

Andi collapsed onto a stool and felt the breath leave her body. She felt as dazed as if someone had punched her in the stomach. "Oh, no. It can't be." She couldn't handle more complications in her life. To discover the money from the recent bank robbery in Fresno *here* under *her* bed was too much.

She dragged one of the sacks across the table and yanked away the coarse ties. When the sack fell open, Andi peered inside and saw gold coins and greenbacks. A *lot* of gold coins and greenbacks. She didn't know what to say.

Jenny had no trouble with her tongue. "It was a crazy, unlikely place to look, I reckon, but I peeked under the bunk to see if there might be an extra store of food. The supplies in this shack are mighty skimpy." She paused and fixed her gaze on the bags. "I saw the sacks and thought they might be full of cornmeal or rye flour, something we could use to rustle up breakfast. But the sacks were so heavy. My eyes nearly popped out of my head when I saw what was stamped on them. I hauled all the ones I could find to the table." She wrapped her arms around herself like she was cold, although the fireplace and the sun streaming through the doorway were already warming the cabin.

Andi pulled her eyes from the money and looked up at her friend. "And here I thought everything would be perfect if only Mitch would wake up."

Jenny fell into the chair beside her. "These are from the bank robbery in town a couple weeks ago, aren't they?" She fingered one of the bags nervously. "There's a heap o' money here, Andi. Probably thousands of dollars. And"—her gaze darted to the open doorway—"those two dead fellas outside are . . ."

"Are most likely the bank robbers," Andi finished, feeling as sick as Jenny looked. She laid her arms across the table, buried her head, and tried to think. Something was not right. She cast her thoughts back to the day of the robbery. *We were in jail. Justin showed up to bail us out. Mr. Washburn rushed in and told the deputy that two men were robbing the bank. Or was it three?* She shook her head. Mr. Washburn had blurted out his words all in a rush. She couldn't remember. Lifting her head, she asked, "How many bank robbers were there?"

"What?"

"Do you remember how many bank robbers the posse went after?"

Jenny shook her head. "What difference does it make?"

"Well, if it's two bank robbers, then we can breathe easy. Mitch got them both. But if there's another . . ." Her voice trailed off and she returned her gaze to the sacks of stolen gold and money.

Jenny's face blanched. "Do you mean there might be more of those snakes sneaking around?"

Andi shrugged. "I don't know. I hope not." She stood up and wandered over to where Mitch lay, still and white. "To be on the safe side, I think we better hide the gold, and hide it good."

"Why don't we slide it back under the bunk and forget we ever saw it?"

Andi felt her temper blaze for an instant, not against Jenny but at the thought of a low-down, good-for-nothing thief getting away with the bank's money. Why! Some of the money in those sacks might belong to her family. "What if there really is a third bank robber and he comes back to get his gold? Would you let him have it without a fight?"

Jenny sighed. "I reckon not."

Andi stood and lifted a sack. "Follow me, Jenny. I just thought of a perfect place to hide it."

Ten minutes later all but two of the sacks lay buried deep inside the pile of hay behind the cabin. "Who'd think to look in such a common spot as a haystack?" Andi asked as she ducked inside to retrieve the final bags. "They'd expect someone to hide treasure in a much better place."

"I hope we've hidden it for no good reason," Jenny replied, grabbing a sack. She slung it over her shoulder. "Two bank robbers are more than enough for me."

Andi was about to agree when Mitch uttered a low moan. Andi dropped the sack she was holding and dashed across the room to her brother's side. His face was twisted in pain, and he didn't open his eyes. "Mitch? You awake?"

She laid a hesitant hand on his forehead. He felt hot, but not dangerously so. Dipping a rag in the pan of water she and Cory had used during the night, she wrung it out and laid it across his forehead. "Please wake up," she begged.

Jenny came and stood behind her. "Give it some time, Andi." She hiked her sack of bank money higher and said, "I'll finish up with these so you can tend to Mitch."

Andi nodded without turning around.

It may or may not have been in answer to her plea, but Mitch's eyelids fluttered. He tossed his head and mumbled, "Thirsty." The rag fell into Andi's hands.

It was one faint word, but Mitch had spoken! Andi's heart leaped with hope. She scrambled to the bucket and dipped out a cup of cool, fresh water. With trembling hands she brought it to her brother, then stopped. How would she ever pour a cup of water down his throat? He lay flat on his back, and it looked like he was unconscious again. But he needed the water, and Andi was determined to get the liquid inside him—no matter what.

But how? She set the cup down, slipped her hand behind his neck, and tried to lift his head. It lolled from side to side, and the water she put to his mouth trickled down his chin and soaked his shirt. Not a drop passed his dry, cracked lips.

"Come on, Mitch. Wake up. Take a drink." He didn't twitch.

Andi let his head fall back on the pillow and sat back to think. Her gaze fell on the rag lying in the pan of water. She'd used it to wash his face and keep him cool, but might it have another use? She lifted the water-soaked rag and laid it against Mitch's lips. Gently, she squeezed the water between his lips and waited. Even unconscious, his mouth sucked at the cloth and his throat worked. Again and again she filled the rag and dribbled the liquid past his lips.

Jenny peered over her shoulder. "Why don't you dump the water on his head? That ought to bring him around."

Andi jumped and dropped the rag. "Don't sneak up on me."

"I wasn't sneaking. I was hiding the gold. I'm done now." She picked up the rag and tossed it in Andi's lap. "It worked last night. If he wakes up, he'll drink a lot more water than the way you're giving it to him."

Andi looked at her brother's pale face. *Now why didn't I think of that?* Aloud she said, "The shock might not be good for him."

"There's one way to find out." Without waiting for Andi's say-so, Jenny lifted the pan of water and emptied part of it over Mitch's head, soaking the pillow and bedding in her eagerness to help.

Jenny's cocky plan had the desired effect. Mitch's eyes flew open and he gasped. He raised a shaky hand and wiped the water from his face. Blinking, he looked around and rasped, "Thirsty."

He stayed conscious long enough to drain three tin cups of water. He gulped them down and lay back with a groan. "Thanks." He closed his eyes.

Andi's joy knew no bounds. She grabbed Jenny and squeezed her tight. "Thank you, Jenny. Your plan worked. He's going to be all right." She closed her eyes and whispered, "Thank you, God," and untangled herself from Jenny's embrace. "Now that Mitch can swallow, he needs more than water in him. How about we cook up some kind of soup or broth or something?" She snatched the black pot and peered inside. "Did you scour this thing real good?"

Jenny held out her hand. "I sure did. Let me fill it from the creek while you decide exactly what *kind* of hearty soup you intend to cook for your brother."

Andi's smile faded. What kind of soup? If she had a trout, she'd boil it, and wouldn't fish soup taste good! Her mouth watered thinking about a nice, fat, fresh trout. A sharp pain ripped through her insides. She pressed a hand against her empty belly. "When did we eat last?"

She tried to remember. Was it yesterday? She'd eaten a quick piece of jerky with Jenny by the boulder, but had she eaten anything since? She didn't think so. No wonder her stomach hollered when her thoughts turned to food. Up until this minute, she'd been too tired and scared to worry about eating.

"Uh . . . I think we ate yesterday," Jenny said. She set the pot down on the table and kneeled beside the bundles Cory and she had stacked against the wall the night before. "Let's see what we've got to make soup. While you cook up the sick man's brew, I'll fix you and me some real food." She wrinkled her nose. "Broth is not on *my* menu this morning." She rummaged through the camping supplies until she came to a burlap sack. Gingerly, she held it out to Andi. "What about this?"

Andi bit her lip and took the sack from Jenny. She didn't have to look inside to know it held Cory's rattlesnake. She counted backward. The snake was two days old. She swallowed. "Plenty of good meat on it, I reckon. Mitch needs broth made with meat, but . . ."

"But what?"

"You can't toss it in the pot like it is. You have to . . . uh, skin it first. And it's not too fresh any longer. I don't think I'm up to that. I feel sick enough as it is." She swallowed again. "If I must, then I'll clean it, but not before we go through every sack and try to find something more appetizing."

That decided, the girls got to work and spread out the remainder of their supplies on the table. There was hardtack, a few cans of beans, flour for biscuits, baking powder, a can of lard, a few potatoes, some apples, and beef jerky. Pounds of beef jerky. There was coffee too, but Andi didn't consider coffee a food choice.

"I reckon it's a toss up between the rattlesnake and the jerky." Andi made a face. She hated jerky. It was tough and stringy, too salty, and chewing it made her jaw hurt. But it was beef. Good, solid, nourishing beef and a far sight better in her mind than skinning and cutting up a two-day-old rattlesnake. Besides, Mitch would be drinking the broth, not Andi.

"The jerky's got my vote," Jenny said with a grin. She grabbed the pot and headed out the door. "I'll be back before you know it."

The girls divided the rest of the long morning and even longer afternoon between keeping the fire going and the broth cooking, trying to wade through the rubbish inside the shack, and scrubbing the grime from the cooking utensils. They gathered old cans and empty whiskey bottles and carried them outside, where they piled them behind the cabin, out of sight. Jenny hauled in two more armloads of firewood to keep the blaze going. Andi stirred her jerky soup creation. Mitch roused off and on through the day, asking for water.

By dusk, Andi and Jenny had completed their tasks. The supplies—both from their own gear and what they'd scrounged from around the shack—had been stacked on shelves, the saddlebags and bundles from the packhorses heaped in a corner out of the way, and the garbage disposed of. The shack had finally aired out, and the scent of Jenny's pan biscuits had replaced the stench from the day before.

Fighting overwhelming weariness, Andi went outdoors to tend the horses. She was bone-tired. She had never worked so hard in her life. She whistled for Taffy, and the faithful mare responded with an answering nicker. She nuzzled Andi while the other horses jostled for attention. A nip here, an irritated whinny from Patches, and the horses settled down.

Andi fed and watered the animals, stroked Taffy's nose one more time, and turned to leave. Taffy tossed her head and stamped a hoof.

"Sorry, Taffy," Andi said, "I'm all done in. You wouldn't believe the things I did today. I've no time to spend with you tonight."

She fetched a bucket of water from the creek and returned to the cabin, where she was greeted with the strong, rich odor of simmering beef broth. "It smells real good," she told Jenny as she set the pail of water on the now-cleared table. Curls of steam rose from the pot hanging over the crackling fire. "This place looks almost cozy. If only . . ." Andi glanced at her brother and bit back what she was going to say.

Jenny sat at the table, picking at a sad-looking helping of beans and a leftover biscuit from lunch. "Go 'head and try the soup, Andi. It's been simmering all day. It's got to be ready by now."

Andi dipped a large spoon in the soup. She stirred the broth and was pleased to see that the water had turned a dark brown. Chunks of jerky floated in the liquid. Smiling, she lifted the spoon and took a sip.

"Oh!" Her eyes smarted, and she coughed. The broth spewed from her mouth. Tossing the spoon aside, she dashed to the bucket and swallowed gulp after gulp of cool water. "It's horrible. I think we threw in too much jerky. It's so salty it'll curl your toes."

"Your brother's not likely to care," Jenny said matter-of-factly, "and you can always add more water to thin it down. Anyways, it's all we've got for him right now."

Jenny spoke the truth. Mitch didn't appear up to eating real food. Who cared how the broth tasted so long as it was nutritious and Mitch drank it?

Andi poured a couple dipperfuls of fresh water into the broth, stirred it around, and drew out a cup of the liquid. When it had cooled, she sat down beside Mitch and motioned Jenny over to help prop him up. "Well, big brother," she said, "this doesn't taste so good, but it's all we've got for now."

To Andi's astonishment, Mitch went after the concoction like a starving man. He guzzled down not only one cup of broth but two more. Although he said nothing, he opened his eyes, wrapped his fingers around the cup, and drank it down with no help. He washed it down with two cups of water and fell back to the bed. But he didn't close his eyes. He looked up at Andi and said, "I think I might make it, after all."

Happy tears sprang to Andi's eyes. At last! After a full day and night of terror, blood, uncertainty, and weariness, Mitch sounded like himself. Andi wanted to hug him tight, but she was afraid of hurting him. Instead, she picked up his hand and squeezed it. "You're going to be fine, Mitch. Just fine."

"And we can all get a good night's sleep," Jenny added with a yawn.

Andi laughed at her friend's practical remark, but inside she let out a sigh of relief. She was so tired. Barring any mishap, a good night's sleep would be welcome indeed.

Chapter Thirteen

SCREAMS IN THE NIGHT

Like a true friend, Jenny offered Andi her spot on the top bunk. "Listen, Andi," she insisted when Mitch had fallen into what looked like a normal, relaxed sleep, "you can't spend another night squished into a tiny ball at your brother's feet. I slept tolerably well last night while you and Cory were tending Mitch. It's your turn for a real bed tonight." She jerked her chin toward the fireplace. "We've been sleeping on the ground for nearly a week, and one more night won't hurt me in the least."

Andi looked with longing at the bunk above her brother. She wanted nothing more than to stretch out on a mattress and sleep for hours and hours. Now that her stomach was full, and with Mitch on the mend, she realized how weary she was in mind and body. But she couldn't let Jenny sleep on the floor.

She shook her head. "It's only been a few days since your own injuries. You take the bunk one more night. Cory will be back with help by tomorrow night, and I'll take my turn then."

Jenny turned stubborn. "Nuthin' doing. You've shouldered a big share of the work and worry around here. I'm just a burr that latched on for the ride, and I feel pretty useless most of the time. My head's fine." To prove her words, she tore the bandage from her head and spun around. "Take a look."

Andi reached out and parted Jenny's red tangles, which were stiff with old, dried blood. It took some doing to see the wound, but to Andi's relief the swelling had gone down. A dark scab was the only sign that Jenny had been hurt. She shrugged and let go. "I reckon you're right, Jenny. I can hardly see it. Mrs. Simmons did a good job fixing you up."

"I haven't had a headache since last night, either," Jenny added. "A good night's sleep will do wonders for you, Andi."

Andi was too tired to argue any longer. After a quick trip outside in the dark to the privy, she climbed to the top of the bunk. She leaned over the side and whispered, "Good night, Mitch," even though she knew he couldn't hear her.

Jenny blew out one kerosene lamp and turned the other down until the light shone barely more than a lit match. She stretched out in front of the dying fire, clasped her hands behind her head, and said, "Good night, Andi."

Andi rolled onto her back and sighed. It felt good not to worry about anything for a change. She listened. It was so still she could hear the breeze rustling the tops of the pines. The creek gurgled. Far away she heard the lonely yip of a coyote. Her eyelids drooped. She only had to get through one more day. Cory would be back tomorrow with Mrs. Simmons and the others to take over.

God, please give me the strength to make it through one more day . . .

Andi's eyes flew open. Cold chills raced up and down her spine. What had awakened her? She lay still, afraid to move, straining her ears for the smallest noise. The creek's familiar bubbling and soft snores from the bunk below were the only sounds Andi heard. Neither explained what had caused her to jerk awake in such fear.

Heart thumping, she rolled over and peered around the cabin. The dim glow of the kerosene lamp showed Jenny sprawled in front of the dead fire, fast asleep. Whatever had yanked Andi from a deep sleep had not affected Jenny or Mitch. Maybe it was only a bad dream.

And why not? Everything that had happened during the last couple of days had given Andi's imagination plenty of ideas for nightmares. *A dream. That's all it was*, she told her galloping heart. She closed her eyes and willed herself to relax and go back to sleep.

The next moment a low, screaming moan pierced the night. Andi jerked up in bed, slamming her head against the low ceiling. But the pain was forgotten as the moaning turned to soul-wrenching cries, loud and insistent. Andi's heart leaped to her throat. Somebody was outside! A woman—sobbing her heart out—lost, alone, and obviously terrified. How could that be? They were miles away from any people. Andi dived under the scanty covering and shook.

"Andi?" Jenny whispered from below. "W-what was that?"

Andi had no idea what the terrible screaming moans might mean, nor did she know who or what had made them. Tears welled up, and she buried herself deeper under the blanket. With all her heart she wished she were home in her own bed, under mounds of fluffy quilts, rather than cowering under a thin covering that barely kept her warm. After this, thunder and lightning storms would hold no fears for her. This noise was a hundred times worse.

"Come down here," Jenny pleaded.

Andi's throat was too tight to answer. With her blood turning to ice and her hands shaking, she threw back the blanket and felt her way down from the bunk. She tiptoed to the lamp and turned up the light. As she did, another piercing scream filled the cabin. This time it sounded close—right outside. The sobbing ripped through Andi's heart. Gasping, she dived to the floor next to Jenny.

Jenny's teeth chattered. "Somebody's in t-terrible trouble. You don't suppose a woman's lost? Should we go outside and f-find her?"

Andi's heart went cold at the thought of going outdoors in the dark, with that dreadful, sobbing noise drawing near. She shook her head. "Not for all the gold in California will I go out there. They'll have to fend for themselves."

As if in protest, the crying and moaning grew louder. Then a new, more frightening sound began. The horses! They were whinnying and snorting in what sounded like unreasoning terror. Whoever or whatever was out there now appeared to be after the horses.

"Taffy!" Andi choked back a sob, but she didn't move. Not even for her precious mare would she venture outdoors to see what was happening. Her stomach turned over.

Jenny gripped her arm. "What should we do?"

Andi didn't know what to do. But she knew someone who did. She raced across the room and laid a trembling hand on her brother's shoulder. She didn't want to wake him, but this new, unknown danger was too much to face alone.

She shook him. "Mitch! You gotta wake up." No response. She shook him again, rougher. "Mitch!"

Mitch's eyes flew open. He stared at Andi as if he didn't recognize her and spoke in a quick, desperate voice. "They're coming. We've got to get out of here."

Andi gaped at her brother, the moaning forgotten for the moment. "What? Why?" She started to back away.

Mitch's eyes darkened in terror. "Hurry!" He clamped strong fingers around Andi's arm and yanked. "Who are you?" he demanded. "What have you done with the others? Tell me!" Each question was accompanied by a rough shake, which set Andi's head jerking.

"Stop it, Mitch! Let me go." Frantic, she planted both feet on the floor and ripped away from his grasp. She tumbled to the floor with a *thud* and scuttled across the room, whimpering in fear and pain.

Jenny wrapped her arms around Andi and whispered. "It's all right, Andi."

"What's wrong with him?" She rubbed her bruised arm and watched her brother from a safe distance as he raved against imaginary enemies. She didn't dare approach him, not even when he fell back and called out for water. He was dangerous—and strong enough to hurt her badly, even in his weakened state.

"He's out of his head," Jenny said. "He's dreaming. It sounds like a bad one. Give him a minute to wake up. He's had a rough time of it, so you can't blame him for acting crazy once or twice." She patted Andi on the shoulder. "Don't worry. Mitch'll be fine once he remembers where he is."

Jenny was right. Mitch stopped tossing and muttering. He let out a long, shuddering breath and turned his head. He flicked his gaze from Andi to Jenny and back to Andi. "What's wrong?"

Andi didn't answer. She didn't have to. A desperate whinny and a piercing, moaning scream made Mitch's eyes grow wide. Instantly his expression turned alert. Whatever nightmare he had experienced was quickly pushed to the back of his mind. "It's a cat," he said grimly. "Sounds like a big one."

"A . . . a cat?" Andi swallowed. "You mean a mountain lion?" The very thought sent Andi's heart racing again. "But it sounds like . . ." She let her voice trail off. Her cheeks burned. Of course no real person would be wandering around at night in the middle of nowhere, screaming and sobbing. What was she thinking? She suddenly felt like a greenhorn, a city-slicker, a fool.

Mitch was nodding. "Big cats scream that way. It makes a person's blood run cold to hear it, especially in the dark, in the middle of the wilderness. Don't feel badly, Andi," he added at the look on her face, "if you've never heard one, it's easy to think it's a poor, lost soul."

Jenny gulped, "I was all ready to rush out and rescue somebody." She broke into nervous laughter. "Born and raised in the woods, and I've never heard a cougar scream . . . thankfully."

The horses' frantic whinnies sliced through their conversation. Andi paled, knowing a mountain lion was out there, perhaps stalking Taffy or one of the other horses. "The cat's after the horses, Mitch. What are we going to do?" Her gaze darted to the rifle propped in the corner next to the door. "We can't let it get Taffy or the others." As much as she dreaded going out there, facing a mountain lion sounded easier than facing the unknown. At least a cat was something she could shoot at. She hurried to the corner and picked up the rifle.

The screaming moan came again. *Then again, maybe not.* She clutched the rifle but knew she could not go out there in the dark.

"You're not going anywhere, with or without the rifle," Mitch said. He lay quietly on the bunk. "We're safe inside this shack. The cat can scream and holler as much as it likes, but it can't get inside."

"But what about the horses?" Andi couldn't bear the thought of Taffy becoming a meal for a hungry mountain lion.

Mitch twisted his head and looked around the cabin. "Is that a window?"

Andi nodded.

"Stick the rifle out and fire off a couple rounds. That should scare our friend away and teach him to stay away from our horses." He paused and listened. The sounds had faded. "But it might be too late."

Andi made her way to the one tiny opening in the shack. She shoved the rifle halfway out the window and pulled the trigger. The sound was deafening in the night and made her ears ring. She fired another round, then one more for good measure. She heard the scuffling and jostling of the horses, a few frightened whinnies, and then silence.

Shaking, she pulled the rifle inside and laid it on the table.

"Good work," Mitch said. "That should keep the cat away, unless it's starving."

"You mean it might come back?" Jenny squeaked.

"I doubt it, but you never know. It doesn't matter, girls. We're safe inside. I suggest we get some sleep. I know I can't keep my eyes open another minute. If I could have a drink of water, I'd be grateful."

While Jenny hurried to give Mitch a cup of water, Andi sat down on the bench beside the table. She yawned. First Mitch. Now the horses. Would there ever come a time when she didn't have to take care of anyone or anything and she could simply rest?

Apparently not. "I'm staying up in case that cat comes back," she announced. "I'll poke the rifle out the window as many times as I need to keep him away. That mountain lion will have to find a meal someplace else. He won't be feasting on any Carter horses if I can help it." She set her jaw when she saw Mitch's look of protest. "Sorry, big brother, but you're too sick to make me do anything else." She placed her hand on the cold, hard rifle barrel and gave him a grim smile. "I'm the boss now."

Chapter Fourteen

THE THIRD SNAKE

I can't take much more of this, Andi thought when she opened her eyes the next morning. To her dismay, she discovered that she had fallen asleep leaning over the table sometime during the night. She felt stiff and sore and worn out. If the mountain lion had returned, she hadn't heard it. Stifling a yawn, she rose from her uncomfortable sleeping position and tried to stretch the stiffness from her limbs. The fire was dead, but she was too tired to coax it back to life.

Treading softly so as not to wake Jenny or Mitch, Andi stepped to the door and cautiously opened it. The sun had already climbed over the mountains and bathed the clearing in warm, golden light. Looking around, she didn't think it possible that she had been so frightened the night before. The day seemed new and fresh and free of danger. Had there really been a mountain lion roaming around during the night? Or had she dreamed the entire thing?

She headed for the corral to check on Taffy—and stopped short. In the soft dust around the cabin and stretching clear to the corral, Andi saw the tracks. They were bigger than a grown man's hand, and they were everywhere. She caught her breath, and her heart thumped wildly. She glanced around for the huge animal that had made its mark. "Don't be silly," she told herself. "It's gone. Don't act like a scared ninny and run screaming back to the cabin."

Little by little, her heart returned to normal, but her mouth stayed dry and her ears listened for the faintest noise. A jay gave a raucous morning cry, and Andi jumped. She chided herself and hurried to the corral, calling Taffy's name.

Taffy trotted up to the fence, along with Mitch's horse Chase, and Patches. The two packhorses, as well as the strangers' horses, were nowhere in sight. The reason why made Andi's mouth drop open and a cold chill enter her bones. The far portion of the corral fence was in shambles, broken clean through.

Andi groaned. The cat must have terrorized the horses into such a frenzy that they'd knocked down the corral fence and run off. The better-trained and more loyal saddle horses had either returned or never left in the first place. Whatever the reason, Andi was grateful. Perhaps the other horses would return if they couldn't find forage in the forest. She hoped none had become the mountain lion's meal. At this point, however, there wasn't much she could do about it if one had. The important thing was that Taffy was safe.

"Bad night, wasn't it, girl?" She rubbed between Taffy's soft ears and planted a kiss on her nose. Then she climbed to the top of the rough corral railing and wrapped her arms around Taffy's neck. The mare stood perfectly still and let Andi nearly choke her in her embrace. "I am so tired of being scared. I feel like we've been here for two months instead of two days. I want to go home, and I bet you do too."

She released Taffy and glanced at the narrow trail that ran past the shack. "Cory should be bringing help sometime today. What a relief that will be. But for now"—she jumped to the ground and gave her horse a final pat—"I'll get you some hay." Then she sighed. "I reckon Jenny and I will have to fix that fence." The thought of more work made her want to curl up in a ball and hide in a corner.

When she returned to the shack, Jenny was up, blowing on the tiny flames that licked the kindling. At the sound of Andi's footsteps, she turned around. "Is . . . is everything all right out there?" Her wide brown eyes asked the real question—*are the horses safe?*

"The horses I can see are fine," Andi replied, "but the packhorses took off through a break in the fence." She lowered her voice. "There are tracks all over the place, but no sign of the mountain lion."

"I should hope not!" Jenny let out a deep breath. "You reckon it'll come back tonight?"

Andi shook her head. "Even if it does, I wouldn't worry. Cory will be here with the men, and they can keep watch." A yawn overtook her. "I plan to sleep all night long tonight."

Jenny grinned and returned to the fire. Andi fetched a bucket of water from the creek. Soon a hot, crackling fire had heated the beef jerky broth for another day, and Jenny was stirring up a batch of pan biscuits for breakfast.

Andi went through the motions of checking Mitch's gunshot wound, but just like she figured, not a drop of blood had leaked out from behind the belt and bandage arrangement. She heard a low whistle and looked up. Mitch was staring at his leg.

"First time I've seen this up close and in my right mind," he remarked.

"It's not pretty," Andi said with a wry grin.

"It looks mighty fine to me, sis." Mitch flopped his head back onto the pillow. "It still feels like a hot poker is stabbing me, but I don't think it's infected, thank God."

"Must have been all that whiskey Cory dumped on it. You stank like a cheap saloon the entire night."

"How would you know what a cheap saloon smells like?" Mitch teased.

Andi laughed out loud. Her brother was surely feeling better if he had the wits to tease her. She raised a finger and laid down the law. "You can't move around too much or you might start bleeding again. And for sure you can't get up yet . . ." She paused and wondered how her brother would be able to take care of any . . . well . . . personal needs if he couldn't even get out of bed. She swallowed. There were a hundred things she could talk to Mitch about, but this was not one of them. It was a good thing Cory and the men would be back soon.

"I'm happy to lie here and think about being alive," Mitch said. He reached out and took her hand. "I knew you could do it, Andi. You just needed a little prodding to get the job done."

"You call scaring me half to death a *little* prodding?"

Mitch dropped her hand. "It worked, didn't it? My leg might not look pretty but it will heal, thanks to you and your friends." He paused. "I should be furious that you didn't stay put like I told you to, but now I'm glad you didn't. Did you fire that shot?"

"Cory did. I wanted to holler, but he wouldn't let me. That fella on the outcropping was fixing to—"

"Yeah, I figured it out," Mitch said. "It's over and done with. Now"—he set his jaw—"I'm going to sit up on my own and eat." He steadied his hands on either side and pushed. His face twisted in pain, but he scooted a bit more. Andi reached out a hand, but he shoved her help aside.

Andi bit her lip.

Slowly, with sweat running down his forehead, Mitch propped himself up and leaned back against the wall, panting with the effort. "Is there anything to eat around here?" he finally asked.

Andi let out the breath she'd been holding and headed for the black pot hanging over the fire. "Jerky soup."

"Sounds good."

"You won't think so now that you're well enough to taste it," Andi said as she poured some into a cup. "But if you drink it down like a good boy I'll give you something that will stick to your ribs better than broth."

Mitch finished the broth in five gulps, wiped his mouth, and grimaced.

"I told you so," Andi said with a laugh. She set a plate of hot biscuits on his lap. "I made some coffee, too. It's probably stronger than you like, but it's good and hot."

Mitch propped himself up higher and accepted the cup of coffee.

He took a sip and grinned. "You're right. It's strong and hot, exactly how I like it. It beats the jerky broth by a long shot."

By the time Andi and Jenny had cleaned up the dishes, straightened the shack, brought in more wood, and fixed the corral fence as best they could, it was nearly noon. Andi slapped the dirt from her hands and shook her head. "A day-old foal could walk through this without missing a step."

"I think the horses will stay put," Jenny said. "Plenty of hay, plenty of water, a little shade. What more could a horse want on a hot day?" It was true. Taffy, Patches, and Chase seemed perfectly content to stand around in the warm sunshine with half-closed eyes and swish flies with their tails.

Mitch was awake and waiting to talk to them when Andi and Jenny tumbled into the shack—hot, hungry, and tired. "You may be the boss of my care, Andi," he said, "but Mother will skin me alive if you work yourself sick on my account. She told me to go easy on you girls, and I've done a mighty poor job of it. I want you both to take a break and get some rest. No arguments," he added when Andi opened her mouth to protest.

Andi nodded in silent relief. Without a word she climbed to the top bunk and spread out on the lumpy, straw-filled mattress. She sighed. It felt so good to let Mitch take over, even a little. *Now that Mitch is out of danger, perhaps Jenny and I can do some fishing this afternoon,* she thought dreamily. *Trout for supper. No more beans and jerky. No more hardtack or biscuits.*

Her worries were finally over. Even the half dozen sacks of hidden gold had been pushed into a little-used corner of her mind. As she drifted off to sleep she remembered that she hadn't told her brother about the bank "treasure" they'd stumbled on. *I'll tell him later . . .*

Later came all too soon. Andi felt she'd been asleep for only a few minutes when she heard the door crash open. She sat up, rubbed her eyes, and glanced down to see Jenny smiling and holding up a string of two good-sized trout.

"About time you woke up, sleepyhead. I've had a fine time fishing the past two hours. It's late afternoon, and these trout will be just the thing for supper. Mitch can have one, and you and I can share the other."

Wide awake, Andi scrambled down from the bunk. Her stomach growled at the sight of the fish. She wasn't even annoyed that she'd slept away the entire afternoon and had missed the chance to wade in the creek and fish with her friend.

"Let's get these cleaned and fried up," Andi said. Grinning, she pulled a pocketknife from her overalls and held it up. "Shall we see who can clean trout the quickest?"

"You bet," Jenny agreed in a flash. She whipped a knife from her own pocket. "We can do it down by the creek."

Andi glanced at Mitch, but he appeared to be asleep. "The smell of trout frying will wake him up faster than all our hollering," she said. "Come on, let's go."

Without warning, a shadow fell across the doorway, blocking the light. Andi blinked. Someone was standing in the opening. She caught her breath and stared at the figure of a man. Then she gasped.

"Deputy Baker!" Her heart leaped. She was so glad to see another adult that she almost hugged Hugh, even though he'd arrested her and her friends. If he brought Mitch safely out of the mountains, she *would* hug him. She smiled. "I'm mighty glad to see you."

Hugh's gaze darted from Andi to Jenny and then rested on Mitch, lying on the bunk. He pulled a pistol from his holster. "I reckon your joy at seeing me won't last long," he sneered.

Andi's smile vanished. What was he saying? Why would he point a gun at her? "I . . . I don't understand. Where's Cory? Where are

Mrs. Simmons and the other men to help my brother? He's been shot."

Hugh grinned. "I know. I met a young fella on the trail. He told me all about it." He stepped away from the doorway, picked up the end of a rope, and gave it a vicious yank. Cory, hands bound and with a gag in his mouth, stumbled into view. Hugh gave him a shove, and Cory fell to the floor with a loud grunt.

"Cory!" Andi and Jenny shrieked.

Andi dumped the trout and her knife on the table and fell to Cory's side. Quick, hot anger burned in her belly at the sight of her friend tied up and hurt. Cory's cheek was scraped and bruised. One eye was nearly swollen shut. *Why would Hugh do such a thing?* She tore at the rope cutting into his wrists.

An ironlike grip on her shoulder shoved her aside. "Leave him be," Hugh growled. "I'll untie him when he's learned some manners." He rubbed a dark bruise on his chin and winced. Obviously, Cory had landed a hard punch to Hugh's face.

Andi lay where Hugh had pushed her, breathing hard. She couldn't wrap her mind around what was happening—Hugh with a gun, Cory tied up. It made no sense. She threw a desperate look at Mitch. He was awake and watching Hugh through narrow, alert eyes. He didn't say a word.

Andi decided to follow her brother's lead and say nothing. She scrambled to her feet and stood helplessly next to Jenny while Hugh's dark gaze flitted around the room. His eyes narrowed when he saw the rifle in the corner. Holstering his gun, he snatched the rifle, removed the cartridges, and dropped the rifle at Andi's feet. Then he reached into his waistband and drew out a second pistol. Andi recognized it at once. It was Mitch's. Hugh emptied it and tossed it beside the rifle.

"Take these guns out back and toss them into the draw." When Andi didn't move, he pulled out his gun and pointed it at Mitch. "I'll keep big brother in my sights to make sure you hurry back."

Andi's heart skipped a beat, and she dived to pick up the firearms. She raced out the door and around the back of the shack. Then she stopped. A few feet away, safely hidden in the pile of old hay, lay the bank gold. Why not stash the guns in the hay too?

She shook her head. "I can't take the chance. If he figures out I tricked him, there's no telling what he'll do." She didn't know what was wrong with Deputy Baker, but he looked downright serious about putting another hole in Mitch.

Hating what she had to do, she pitched the rifle and pistol over the edge of the gully and listened as the metal clattered against the rocks. The sound echoed through the small canyon, sending shivers up and down Andi's spine. Their only hope of protection was gone, tumbling to ruin at the bottom of the draw.

"What are we going to do *now*?" She choked back a frightened sob.

Unbidden, a Bible verse popped into Andi's head. *God is our refuge and strength, a very present help in trouble.* She peered over the edge of the deep draw. Maybe they didn't need the guns after all. Maybe God wanted her and her friends to use their heads to get out of this fix.

She blinked back tears and mumbled a quick prayer for safety in a world that had suddenly turned upside down.

Chapter Fifteen

A LONG NIGHT

Andi slipped into the cabin and stood by Jenny. No one had moved during her errand. She lifted her chin. "I did what you told me."

"Good for you." Hugh grunted in satisfaction and holstered his pistol. "I don't want to spend the rest of the day with a gun in my hand. If you three behave yourselves, I'll let the boy loose." He turned to Mitch. "I know *you* won't be any trouble, Carter. According to the boy, you about bled to death the other day. I reckon you're pretty much confined to that bed."

Mitch said nothing.

Hugh unsheathed a long, wicked-looking blade and cut through Cory's bonds like they were fine threads. Then he ripped away the gag. Cory sucked in a long, shuddering breath. He looked miserable—beaten, filthy, and defeated. Had it been only yesterday morning when he'd left the cabin with such high hopes of bringing back the help Mitch so desperately needed?

Cory's words confirmed Andi's worst fears. "I'm sorry," he croaked. "I was nearly to town when I met the deputy hurrying up the trail. I was so glad to see him that I told him everything that had happened. I asked him to go into town with me and find help, but he laughed and yanked me off my horse. He snatched the gun away and told me we were going back up in the mountains. I tried to get away, but he did this"—he pointed to his bruised face—"and tied me up. I don't know what's going on, but he's no deputy." Cory scowled at Hugh, showing Andi that he wasn't completely subdued. "He's a weasel, and a disgrace to the badge he used to wear."

During Cory's recital, Hugh had settled his slight frame on the bench near the table and rested his hand lightly on his holster. He didn't deny anything Cory said. Instead, a secretive smile crossed his face. After Cory finished his short tale, Hugh drew a casual breath and said, "The boy's right. I'm not a deputy, and those six long, miserable weeks back in Fresno convinced me that I never want to be. But I drew the short straw, so I got the job." His smile widened. "It worked out just like we planned."

For the first time since Hugh's unexpected arrival, Mitch spoke. "What worked out?" He propped himself up on his elbow and bored into the deputy's eyes with a fierce blue gaze.

Hugh stood and ambled across the room to Mitch's side. "The bank job. I've come for the money." He folded his arms across his chest. "Where is it?"

Utter silence greeted Hugh's words. Cory's mouth fell open. Mitch looked confused.

Andi's heart leaped to her throat. She felt her cheeks flush in sudden realization. Hugh was one of the bank robbers. But that was impossible! He'd been busy arresting Andi and her friends during the bank robbery. He'd formed the posse to track the outlaws. He'd . . .

Andi gasped. Chad's frustrated words from the week before made sense now. *By the time the posse figured out we were on a fool's errand, any real trace of the outlaws had disappeared.*

"You led the posse the wrong way on purpose," she burst out, clenching her fists.

Hugh winked at Andi. "That's right, girl. Soon as Sheriff Tate left town I knew the time had come. I let Rob and Ike know, and they got clean away—like we figured." A brief expression of regret passed over his features, but he brushed it away. "I'm sorry they're dead, but there's no use mourning over what can't be changed. All that gold will give me comfort in my time of sorrow." His smirk told Andi that Hugh was worse than a weasel—he wasn't even loyal to his comrades. "Now, where's the gold?" He addressed his question to Mitch.

"I have no idea," Mitch replied. "I've been unconscious most of the time. I haven't seen or—"

Hugh ripped the blanket from Mitch, raised his fist, and brought it down on the wounded leg. Mitch cried out in agony. His face turned gray.

Andi's fear vanished. The anger she'd felt at seeing Cory trussed up spread to her limbs. She took a flying leap at Hugh and caught him off-balance. Together they tumbled to the floor. Hugh tossed her aside and yanked the gun from his holster.

"Hold it right there."

Andi sat on the floor a few feet away, breathing hard. Jenny and Cory stood across the room, wide-eyed and speechless.

"I told you to behave yourself." He motioned with his gun. "Get over there with the others."

Andi scrambled to obey.

With careful deliberation, Hugh rose to his feet and rested the barrel of his gun against Mitch's good leg. "Now, Mitch Carter, if you don't tell me what I want to know by the time I count to ten, I will put a bullet in your other leg." He took a deep breath and began counting. "One . . . two . . . three . . ." He looked at Andi, who was biting her lip to keep from crying out.

"I can't tell you what I don't know!" Mitch said between gasps.

"Four . . . five . . . six . . ."

"Stop it!" Andi dashed forward with a sob. "He doesn't know where the money and gold are. Please don't shoot him."

Hugh's hand didn't waver. "Seven . . ."

"I"—Andi glanced at Jenny, who nodded—"I know where it is," she finished in a rush.

"Andi!" Mitch groaned. "How . . . ?"

She turned to him, her face wet with tears. "Jenny found it when we were cleaning up yesterday. We hid it, but with everything going on, I forgot to tell you. Maybe if we give him the money, he'll go away and leave us alone."

Cory shook his head in disbelief. "You found the bank money?" He stared at Jenny in awe. "You hid it?" He managed a small grin. "Good for you!"

"Shut up, boy," Hugh ordered. He pulled his gun away from Mitch and waved it toward Andi. "How much is there?"

"About half a dozen sacks," Jenny answered before Andi could speak. She stepped forward. "I'll take you to it if you leave Andi's brother alone."

Hugh slipped his gun back in the holster. "Sure thing, girl. Lead the way. The rest of you come along. You can help me carry the sacks." He turned to Mitch. "I suggest you stay right where you are. I have your sister and her friends, and I'm not afraid to hurt them to get what's mine."

Mitch didn't answer. It was obvious that he wasn't going anywhere. His face was gray, and beads of sweat dotted his forehead. Hugh grunted and followed Jenny out the door.

Five minutes later a pile of sacks lay heaped along the inside wall next to the cabin door. Hugh dropped the last sack on the mound and planted his fists on his hips. He whistled. "That's a heap of gold, for a fact." His eyes gleamed. "Tomorrow morning you can help me pack it up on a horse, and I'll be on my way. By the time any of you go for help, I'll be clean out of these parts."

"Tomorrow?" Andi said. "Why don't we help you pack it up right now?"

Hugh poked his scraggly head out the doorway and squinted at the setting sun. "Nope. There's not enough daylight to get a good start. I'd much rather spend the night in a cabin than on the open trail. You girls have turned this shack into a real cozy little place. Rob and

Ike weren't such good housekeepers." He pointed at Cory. "You, boy, go tend our horses and come right back. If you take off, these girls will pay for your stupidity."

Cory exchanged glances with Andi and Jenny, then disappeared through the open door.

"What's there to eat around here?" Hugh barked. His gaze fell on the forgotten fish lying on the table. Grinning, he picked up one of the trout and motioned to Andi. "I'm starved. What do you say you fry me up these fish?" He turned to Jenny. "And I could really go for some coffee and maybe a biscuit or two."

Andi and Jenny looked at each other. The last thing Andi wanted to do was cook for this miserable snake of a man. She felt sick.

"Hey, I'm talking to you," Hugh roared. He grasped Andi's arm, jerked her toward him, and shoved the fish into her hands. "Fix me something to eat, and do it quick."

Andi clenched her jaw and stood stiffly, holding the fish. She wanted nothing more than to slap him across the face with the scaly fish. She glared at him. *He can starve.*

"Do it, Andi." Mitch's voice broke through her resolve.

Andi's shoulders slumped. She carried the fish to the counter to clean them. She choked back the bile that rose at the thought of cooking the fish meant for Mitch and giving it to a low-down bank robber.

Jenny took Andi's cue and hurried to mix up a batch of biscuits. The way she attacked the dough told Andi that her friend was fit to be tied about what she was being forced to do.

When Cory returned from his chore, the fish were sputtering in the frying pan over the fire and a heavenly odor of baking biscuits wafted up from a covered pan nearby. One look at Andi, and Cory's tentative smile turned to a frown. "I take it that supper's not for us," he said dully.

Andi's stomach rumbled, craving a bite of the trout. She shook her head. Cory sighed and plopped down against the wall to watch and wait.

Hugh sat at the table, clearly enjoying the aroma of his supper. He smacked his lips when Andi dumped the trout and biscuits onto a tin plate. She brought the food to Hugh and dropped it on the table in front of him. The plate clattered, and a biscuit bounced from the dish.

Hugh lashed out and grabbed Andi's wrist. "I like my food served cheerfully."

"Let go of me," she said between clenched teeth, yanking her arm away.

Hugh picked up his fork and pointed it at her. "You're not very friendly, girl. Not friendly at all." He stabbed at a piece of fish and stuffed it in his mouth. "But," he conceded with a smile, "you can cook. I'll give you that."

"I hope it chokes you," Andi mumbled, watching the scene with disgust. She turned back to the meager supplies and helped Jenny dig through cans of beans and packages of hardtack. Looking at her choices, even a hunk of beef jerky sounded good tonight. She heated up a can of beans and snitched a biscuit for Mitch, poured him some coffee, and took it to him.

"Thanks," he said quietly, keeping a wary eye on Hugh.

"Oh, Mitch," Andi whispered, "what are we going to do?"

"Nothing," came his sensible reply. "We're going to let him take the money and leave. The gold's not worth getting hurt over."

"Are you sure he'll leave us here and—?"

"Get away from big brother, girl."

Hugh's gruff command startled Andi, and she whirled. The deputy-turned-outlaw had his gun out, pointing it at her. He motioned her away.

"I don't want any plotting or whispering going on." He pushed back from the table and stood up. "It's getting late, and I've got a long day ahead of me tomorrow. I intend to get a good night's sleep, so I reckon I'll have to do something to keep all of you in one place." Holstering his gun, he rummaged through his gear and drew out a length of rope. "This should do it."

Cory's face paled. "Oh, no, not again. He tied me up last night on the trail. I'm telling you, it's a lousy way to sleep. My arms and back still ache."

"Too bad. That's the way it's gonna be, kids." Hugh smirked. "But first things first." He made his way over to Mitch and said, "Sick or not, I'm tying you up too." He yanked Mitch's hands above his head and tied them securely around the bedpost. Then he stepped back to observe his handiwork. "That should keep you out of trouble."

Andi soon found herself trussed up like a calf waiting to be branded. Lying on the floor in front of a dying fire, with her hands and her ankles cinched tight, she agreed with Cory. This was a lousy way to spend the night.

Hugh blew out the light, and the cabin was plunged into near darkness. Andi heard the creaking of the bunk and realized with a pang of envy that Hugh would be sleeping in a bed tonight while she, Mitch, and her friends lay helpless and hurting. She knew she wouldn't sleep a wink.

A long while later, Andi heard the sound of snoring coming from the top bunk. She hadn't dared whisper to her friends before, but now that Hugh was asleep, maybe—

"Andi!" It was Cory. "Are you awake?"

"Of course I am. How can anybody sleep tied up like this?" She heard a nervous giggle from Jenny at her feet. Carefully, with only the glow of the embers to help her see, Andi scooted and twisted around until she was head to head with her friends.

"What are we going to do?" Jenny wanted to know.

"We can't let that miserable snake run off with our town's gold," Cory hissed. "We've gotta do something."

Andi didn't say anything.

"Andi," Cory said, "I know Mitch told you that we should let Hugh take the money and leave, but hang it all! Some of that money belongs to my folks. Maybe *your* family can afford to let bank robbers run off with your gold, but my pa can't. It'll ruin him."

"I'm with Cory," Jenny put in quietly. "How do we know that skunk is even telling the truth about leaving us here? What's to stop him from taking one of us with him, or worse—shooting us? Mitch can't do a thing about it, laid up like he is. But we can."

"Hugh's got the gun," Andi reminded her reckless friends.

"There're three of us," Cory said.

"Who's volunteering to draw Hugh's fire?"

Silence.

Deep in her heart, Andi knew Mitch was right. The money wasn't worth the danger. But Jenny was right too. Could Hugh be trusted to keep his word about taking the money and letting them go free? The man was a scoundrel—a good-for-nothing, lying crook. He'd bullied Cory and hurt Mitch to get what he wanted. Andi had no doubt he was capable of hurting her and Jenny too. Hugh could not be trusted.

Andi strained her eyes to see through the darkened room. She could barely make out a burlap sack lying forgotten in the far corner under the window. "You're right, Cory. So is Jenny. We need to be ready." She smiled in the dark. "I've got an idea . . ."

Chapter Sixteen

A RECKLESS CHANCE

A tingling pain in her hands woke Andi after a fitful, restless sleep. "Get up," Hugh growled, ripping away her bonds.

Andi ignored both Hugh and the pins and needles in her hands. She curled up in a tight ball without even opening her eyes. The floor was hard but she was so tired. A few more minutes of sleep would be heavenly.

A booted toe jabbed her in the back. "Come on. Get up. I'm starved. Fix me some grub."

Another jab convinced Andi that she'd better obey. She opened her eyes and found herself looking into the fireplace. Her heart felt as cold as the dead ashes. She sat up, groggy and aching. Her only surprise was that she'd actually fallen asleep. Perhaps if she'd stayed awake all night she wouldn't feel so stiff and sore.

Andi looked over at Mitch, who remained tightly bound. He appeared to be asleep.

"I . . ." Andi began, turning back to Hugh.

"What?"

She felt her cheeks flush. "I . . . I need to use the privy," she finished lamely.

"By all means," Hugh consented with a grin. He slid his gun from his holster and laid it on the table. Andi stared at it. "That's a reminder not to dawdle. I'm in a hurry today. I wouldn't want to leave your brother with a matching hole in his other leg. You hear me?"

Andi nodded and fled the cabin. When she returned she saw that

Hugh had cut Jenny's ropes and was standing over her, watching as she rubbed the life back into her numb limbs. Cory, too, was free, coaxing life into the tiny blaze he'd lit in the fireplace. *Hugh is treating us like slaves,* she thought with scorn.

"What about Mitch?" she asked. "You need to let him go."

Hugh shook his head. "He's no use to me this morning. I'll just have to tie him up again when I leave."

Andi's heart froze. "W-what do you mean?"

"You kids will feed me and help me pack up. I'm leaving like I promised but"—Hugh's look turned wary—"I've decided not to take any chances. I'm tying you all up again."

Jenny moaned.

The piece of firewood Cory was holding fell from his hand and landed on the floor with a *thud*. He turned on Hugh. "We'll die!" he shouted up at him. "Haven't you done enough?"

"Take it easy, boy," Hugh said with a gruff laugh, "I won't tie you so tight that you can't eventually get loose. It'll only slow you down some. Now get the fire going so I can eat and be on my way."

Cory's shoulders sagged as he turned back to the fire. Andi wondered how he could stay awake. One night tied up had been uncomfortable. Two nights must have been pure torture for him. She hurried over to lend a hand, but Hugh reached out and snagged her arm as she passed the table.

"I told you to rustle me up some grub, girl. He can tend the fire without your help. You and *you*"—he jabbed a finger in Jenny's direction—"get me something to eat."

Andi tried to twist away from Hugh's grip, but he held her tight.

"What's the matter with you this morning? You're as jumpy as water on a hot skillet. Something on your mind?"

Andi looked into Hugh's cold, gray-flecked eyes. There was plenty on her mind, but nothing she dared tell Hugh. "I don't like being tricked. You said you'd leave. You never said anything about tying us up."

Her answer brought a grin to Hugh's face. He laughed and let her go. "I reckon I left out a detail or two. I apologize. Now fix my breakfast."

Andi turned away and caught Mitch looking at her. There was no way to tell him what she and her friends had planned, so she gave him a cheerful smile and started for the corner under the window.

"You got any fish from yesterday?" Hugh twisted around in his chair and called to Andi. "That was the best trout I ever tasted."

When Andi shook her head, Hugh sighed. "No steak? No eggs? You got anything in those supplies to fill a hungry man's belly?"

Andi bent over and lifted the innocent-looking burlap sack. Her hands were shaking so badly she could barely hang on to it. *Please, God, make this work!* "Actually, I do," she said, trying to keep her voice light and casual. Inside, her thoughts were screaming, *I can't do this. I can't touch it. I feel sick.* She swallowed and hefted the sack over her shoulder. She pasted a smile on her face and walked back to Hugh with a confidence she did not feel. As she passed Mitch, she heard him whisper, "What are you planning?"

She dropped the heavy burlap sack on the table and slowly began to open the top. From the corner of her eye she saw Cory and Jenny alert and watching her every move. "We were saving this as a special treat for our supper the last night we were on the trail."

"No, Andi," Cory cried out. "He's already eaten our trout. You can't let him have this too." He joined Andi at the table, a look of disgust written all over his face. "I've been looking forward to it all week long."

"Shut up, boy!" Hugh demanded. He made a swipe at the sack, but Andi pulled it back. "Whatever it is, get it cooked up quick. My belly's screaming for breakfast."

"Don't you want to see what it is?" Andi asked, eyes wide. She felt small drops of sweat trickle down her neck. Her heart slammed against the inside of her chest like a hammer. When Hugh gave a curt nod, she reached into the sack. Her hand curled around the dry, scaly body of Cory's rattlesnake. It required every ounce of courage she possessed to keep from dropping it and running out the door. She took a deep, steadying breath and grasped the dead reptile tighter. Everything depended on what she did next.

With a mighty heave, Andi yanked the snake from the burlap sack and threw it in Hugh's face. "It's a rattler! Watch out!" she shrieked.

The snake hit its target dead on. Hugh roared his surprise and terror. With flailing arms, he tried to knock the reptile away, but it was no use. He lost his balance, flew backward off the chair, and landed on his back with a yelp. The snake lay across his neck like a cheap, leathery muffler. Cursing, he flung it aside and fumbled at his holster. It was empty.

Andi's triumph at the success of her plan was shattered when Hugh rolled onto his side and stretched out his hand. She tried to skip out of the way, but Hugh was too quick. He caught her by her overalls leg and yanked. With a cry, she fell on top of him.

The next instant Andi felt Hugh's arm locked around her neck. She reached up and dug her fingers into his arm, but she couldn't pull herself free. Hugh rose to his feet, dragging Andi with him. She could feel him shaking, but she was too busy trying to take a breath to wonder how furious he must be at her trick. His choke hold grew tighter. She couldn't speak. She couldn't breathe. The world began to turn black. Andi closed her eyes and felt herself grow limp.

"The gun," Hugh was saying. His voice seemed to come from a long ways off, but he wasn't yelling. Instead, he sounded calm and reasonable. "Give it to me and I'll let her go." He loosened his grip a fraction, and Andi gasped in a lungful of cool, fresh air. She opened her eyes. Cory stood a few yards away, holding the pistol. It was pointed at Hugh.

Cory shook his head. "No. You let Andi go, get on your horse, and clear out of here. The money stays with us."

Hugh's chuckle made Andi cringe. "You're a kid. You won't shoot, especially when I have your friend right where I want her." He lowered his mouth to Andi's ear and whispered, "That was a stupid thing to do, girl. Look where it got you. Any time I want, I can do this"—he tightened his arm—"and that will be the end." He turned back to Cory. "Put the gun on the table and step away." When Cory didn't move, he barked, "Now!"

"Do it, Cory." Mitch's voice rang out from across the room.

Cory lowered the gun to his side and stepped toward the table. "I'm sorry, Andi. I reckon I should have yanked you out of his way before going for the gun." He sighed, laid the pistol carefully on the table, and backed away.

Hugh released Andi, gave her a shove, and reached for his weapon. Then . . .

Clang!

The sound of a large metal object crashing against something solid was the sweetest sound Andi had ever heard. She turned. Jenny stood over a groaning Hugh Baker, holding the cast iron frying pan with both hands. The man lay on the floor, writhing in pain and holding his head.

Cory grabbed the gun. Andi rushed to Mitch's side and began sawing away at his bonds.

"Should I whack him again?" Jenny asked. She looked at Mitch for an answer. "I was sort of hoping to knock him out so he wouldn't be any more trouble."

Mitch sat up, rubbed his wrists, and accepted the gun that Cory thrust into his hand. With slow deliberation, he pulled back on the hammer. It clicked, and Hugh froze. "That won't be necessary, Jenny. I think Hugh knows I mean business when I say he'd better not so much as twitch while Cory ties him up."

Cory scrambled for rope to complete his task. In a few minutes Hugh's hands and ankles were secured. Cory, Andi, and Jenny dragged the helpless man to Mitch's bunk and tied him to a post at the foot of the bed. He hollered and cursed so loudly that Cory found Hugh's bandana and gagged him. "When you can talk politely in the company of ladies, we'll take it off," he said.

From the look on Hugh's face, Andi figured the bandana wouldn't be coming off for a long time.

"Cory," Mitch said when he'd lowered the hammer and set the gun down next to his pillow, "you have to go back to town. I won't bleed to death now, but I'm nowhere near up to climbing on a horse." He winced. "I've got all I can do to keep from passing out every time I move my leg. We can't stay up here forever holding a gun on our bank robber, either. Find Mrs. Simmons and tell her what happened. Ask her to send a wire to Fresno. Then bring back help. If you hurry you can make it by sundown." He lay back and let out a long, tired breath. "The girls and I will take turns staying awake to guard our prisoner."

For the second time in two days, Andi told Cory good-bye. Her friend looked tired but determined as he climbed onto Flash's back and gathered the reins. "This time I'll come back with the help I promised," he said cheerfully. But Andi knew his smile was forced. She wished she could go in his place.

Cory waved and disappeared around the bend. Andi dropped her hand and shuffled into the cabin with a weary sigh. She was sick of this place. She was tired of being hungry and dirty, tired of being scared, and tired of being exhausted all the time. *I want to go home.* Her eyes stung. *No crying!* she ordered herself.

"Andi," Mitch said, "you and Jenny are going to stay outdoors for the rest of the morning. You can fish or pan for gold, or sit by the creek and do nothing." He propped himself up on his elbow and let the weight of Hugh's gun rest in his palm. "You've done more than your share and it's my turn now. Is that clear?"

Andi brightened. She exchanged a look with Jenny, whose face had lit up at Mitch's words. "Really? You'll be all right guarding"—she glanced at Hugh—"him?"

"You bet I will," Mitch assured her with a smile. "Go catch us some dinner."

Andi suddenly didn't feel tired any longer. With a whoop she snatched up her fishing pole and headed out the door. "Come on, Jenny. I'll race you to the creek!"

Chapter Seventeen

REAL TREASURE

Ten days later, Andi eyed Jenny's farewell cake with a calculating look. She raised the knife and hacked off a generous slice. It toppled to the dessert plate in her hand. Crumbs cascaded over the edge and onto the tablecloth. A glob of white frosting covered her fingertips. *Oops.* Andi glanced around. No one had seen the mess she'd made. She put the plate down, licked her fingers, and picked it up again.

"Hmm . . . heavenly." She sighed at the taste of frosting.

"Thanks, little sister." Chad came up behind her and reached for the plate. "Just the size I like."

Andi didn't let go. "This is not for you," she said primly, snatching up a fork and a napkin.

"*You're* eating it all?" He raised his eyebrows. "I know you didn't eat much that week you were stuck in the mountains, but stuffing yourself on cake isn't the best way to make up for it."

Andi brushed by her brother. "If you must know, this piece is for Mitch," she shot over her shoulder. Then she saw Chad's grin. He was teasing her again. Her annoyance melted away, and she smiled at him. She hadn't realized how much she'd missed Chad's bluster and bossiness. She felt like she'd been gone two years rather than the two weeks of their ill-fated camping trip. Now, after arriving safely back on the ranch, things were returning to normal. *At least I'm not waking up with nightmares any longer,* Andi thought with relief.

She made her way to the settee, where Mitch lay with his leg propped up. Cory and Jenny sat nearby on a couple of footstools, eating cake and chatting with him.

"Here, Mitch." Andi handed him the overflowing plate and a napkin. "Chad tried to swipe it, but I brought you the largest piece I could cut."

Mitch held it up. "It's . . . uh . . . big," he finally said.

Jenny giggled.

"We have to fatten you up," Andi explained. She glanced at his leg. "How are you feeling?" It had taken two days for their rescuers to pack Mitch down the mountain to Fresno Flats. Other men had stayed behind to round up the missing horses, bury the dead, pack up the sacks of bank gold, and see to it that Hugh Baker was properly restrained for his trip to jail. From Fresno Flats, it had taken another two days to arrive in Madera and catch the train to Fresno and the ranch. It had been a painful trip home, and Andi had not once left her brother's side.

"I'm fine," Mitch assured her, "I feel the same as when you asked me at breakfast and again at lunch. You saw me hobbling around this morning. It won't be long until I'm back in the saddle and flushing out strays."

Andi plopped down beside him on the settee. "Are you sure? Maybe you should take it easy for—"

"You don't need to hover, sis," Mitch said. He set his cake aside and grasped her hand. "Doc Weaver says I'm past any danger and completely on the mend. He also reminded me that it's thanks to *you*"—he looked past her to include Jenny and Cory—"and your friends that I'm alive. You did something not many could do, Andi. Now stop fretting. You can put all the bad times behind you and go back to being a carefree little girl again." He squeezed her hand. "Isn't that what you want?"

Andi dropped her head. "I reckon." But she wasn't sure. There was nothing quite like knowing that she had saved her brother from certain death and brought him safely home. It made her feel rich inside—richer than if she'd found a three-pound gold nugget in the creek. She felt grown up as well. Perhaps more than she liked, but grown up all the same. Her brother's words from the first night on the trail whispered in her head: *I'd rather have a sensible young woman around—one who can think clearly and do what's got to be done . . .*

Maybe growing up wasn't such a bad idea, after all. She liked the idea of being considered a sensible young woman—even if she'd been scared half to death at the time.

Mitch lifted Andi's chin and smiled at her. "Hey, enough about how I'm doing. This is Jenny's last day on the ranch. Let's make her going-away party one she'll always remember."

Jenny grinned. "It's surely a *visit* I'll always remember. Don't know how I'll ever settle back into everyday life after this." She ticked off their past adventures on her fingers and finished with, "I could have done without the rattlesnake, but it turned out to be a handy critter to keep around, after all." Her smile widened. "I'm mighty glad we didn't eat it."

Andi cringed. She could still feel the snake's dry, heavy weight against her palms.

"I've got an idea, Andi," Mitch added with a sly grin. "You might not be a deadeye with a rifle like that Annie Oakley gal, but I bet you could enter a rattlesnake-throwing contest. You hit your target dead on."

Cory and Jenny howled.

Try as she might to look offended, Andi couldn't hold back her laughter. Before long, Chad, Melinda, and their mother wandered over to find out what was so funny.

"Sounds like I'm missing the party," Justin called from the foyer. He closed the front door and stepped into the parlor wearing a smile. He tossed his hat on an empty table, joined the small crowd around Mitch, and presented Jenny with an envelope. "Your train ticket,

Miss Grant, for the westbound 9:14 to Oakland, tomorrow morning. Mrs. Evans, who is traveling to San Francisco to visit her daughter, has agreed to accompany you and see you safely aboard your ship to Tacoma and the wilderness."

Andi covered her mouth to smother a giggle. Crotchety old Mrs. Evans wasn't the companion Andi would have chosen for an eight-hour train ride to the city. Perhaps she should warn Jenny to slouch in her seat and pretend to be asleep the whole trip. She couldn't tell her now, however. Justin wasn't finished.

He pulled three small packets from his pocket. "There's one for each of you." He handed them to Andi and her friends.

"What is it?" Andi asked. She turned the packet over in her hand.

"Open it," Justin said.

Silence fell over the group while Cory, Jenny, and Andi tore into their envelopes.

Cory was the first to see what fell out. He gasped. "It's money!"

Andi pulled out ten crisp five-dollar bills. "Fifty dollars?" She gaped at her brother. "Why?"

Justin grinned. "It's Charles Wilson's way of saying thank you for bringing back the bank gold and capturing one of the thieves. I've never seen a bank president look so happy or relieved. I bet most of the townsfolk feel the same way. There was a lot of gold and money in those sacks you found." He unfolded a newspaper and held it up. "I also brought home the *Expositor*. Heroes, all of you. The article on the front page of *this* edition is a much better read than the one that ran a few weeks ago, when you three spent time in jail."

Andi sat frozen on the settee, the ten bills laid out on her lap. *This is a lot of money.* She looked at Mitch. "But you took care of a couple of the robbers. Shouldn't you . . . ?"

"You kids earned it," Mitch said. "Accept it gracefully."

Cory's eyes were shining. "You bet I'll accept it." He shoved his hand into the pocket of his trousers and pulled out a small vial of gold flakes and nuggets. "I thought gold would be the treasure I came home with, but it doesn't hold a candle to *this* treasure—fifty whole dollars." He shook his head and stuffed the vial back into his pocket. "I'm rich."

Jenny giggled. "I didn't find any gold, but I'm taking treasure home too." She turned to Andi. "What about you, Andi?"

Andi carefully replaced the money in her envelope and set it aside. "Oh, yes. I came home with treasure, Jenny, but it's not the gold I found or even the fifty dollars reward." She turned and flung her arms around Mitch's neck. "I came home with my brother."

To find out more about Andi and her friends,
visit Andi's blog at www.circlecadventures.com.

To contact Susan K. Marlow, e-mail her at
susankmarlow@kregel.com.

A literature unit study with enrichment activities
is available for *Trouble with Treasure* as a free download at
www.circlecadventures.com.

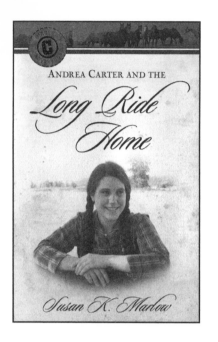

Circle C Adventures Book 1
ANDREA CARTER AND THE LONG RIDE HOME

Twelve-year-old Andi Carter can't seem to stay out of trouble. Now her beloved horse, Taffy, is missing and it's Andi's fault. The daring young girl will do anything to find the thief and recover Taffy. But her choices plunge her into danger, and Andi discovers that life on her own in the Old West can be downright terrifying!

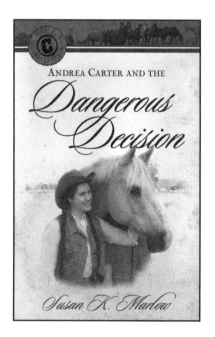

Circle C Adventures Book 2
ANDREA CARTER AND THE DANGEROUS DECISION

Andi nearly tramples her new teacher in a reckless, impromptu horse race down the main street of Fresno, California—not a good way to begin the fall school term. Her troubles multiply when she must decide if she should deliberately walk into a dangerous situation to rescue the teacher's mean-spirited, troublemaking daughter.

Circle C Adventures Book 3
ANDREA CARTER AND THE FAMILY SECRET

W hy had Andi never been told the secret her family has carefully kept hidden? Angry and hurt at being left out, Andi saddles Taffy and sets out to find some answers—answers that turn her world upside down. How far must Andi go to rescue those she loves and whose lives depend on her protection?

Circle C Adventures Book 4
ANDREA CARTER AND THE SAN FRANCISCO SMUGGLERS

W hen a winter flood in Fresno closes school temporarily, Andi is sent to live with an aunt in San Francisco, doomed to finish the winter term of school at Miss Whitaker's Academy for Young Ladies. There Andi; her roommate, Jenny; and Lin Mei, a young girl who works at the school, discover a disturbing secret. Soon these new friends find themselves in more trouble than they can handle.